The GiRL

WHO FELL OUT OF THE

SKY

A FEIWEL AND FRIENDS BOOK

An imprint of Macmillan Publishing Group, LLC

120 Broadway, New York, NY 10271

Our books may be purchased in bulk for promotional, educational, or business use.
Please contact your local bookseller or the Macmillan Corporate and Premium
Sales Department at (800) 221-7945 ext. 5442 or by email at
MacmillanSpecialMarkets@macmillan.com.

Library of Congress Cataloging-in-Publication Data.

Library of Congress Cataloging-in-Publication Data

Names: Forester, Victoria (Victoria Lakeman), author.
Title: The girl who fell out of the sky / Victoria Forester.
Description: First edition. | New York : Feiwel and Friends, 2020. | Summary:
    When Piper loses her ability to fly, she finds she cannot even do ordinary things
    until the "normal" people around her help her recover her abilities, as she
    discovers theirs.
Identifiers: LCCN 2019018303 | ISBN 9781250089311 (hardcover)
Subjects: | CYAC: Ability—Fiction. | Individuality—Fiction. |
    Flight—Fiction. | Self-acceptance—Fiction. | Science fiction.
Classification: LCC PZ7.F75873 Giv 2020 | DDC [Fic]—dc23
LC record available at https://lccn.loc.gov/2019018303

ISBN 978-1-250-08931-1 (hardcover) / ISBN 978-1-250-08932-8 (ebook)

Feiwel and Friends logo designed by Filomena Tuosto

First edition, 2020

1   3   5   7   9   10   8   6   4   2

VICTORIA FORESTER

THE GIRL WHO FELL OUT OF THE SKY

FEIWEL AND FRIENDS

NEW YORK

CHAPTER

1

JIMMY JOE MILLER SUCKED ON A STALE piece of gum and dangled his baseball bat between his hands. Keeping to the thin shade cast off by the awning of Jameson's Dry Goods and Feed, he squinted his eyes and surveyed Main Street—not a soul to be seen.

There wasn't much to do on a stinking hot day like this in Lowland County, and Jimmy Joe was out scavenging for a boy his size or smaller with a mind to play ball. Of course, he could ask one of his four older brothers, but being the youngest meant they always bested him, and Jimmy Joe wanted to win. It wasn't fun when you lost all the time, and it rankled him when they teased, which they did without mercy.

Taking the tip of his tongue, he fussed at his gum and then blew into it. A plump bubble took shape as a horsefly buzzed up, bothering him. In no time flat,

Jimmy Joe was swinging his bat wildly at it, his face puffing and red.

"What in Sam Hill are you doing?" said a voice, unexpectedly coming out of nowhere.

Startled, Jimmy Joe dropped his bat and spun around to discover a girl inches behind him.

He didn't like the look of this girl. She had sharp blue eyes that were hard to turn away from. Also, she was messy. She had on a pair of worn blue jeans with a rip over the left knee, and her T-shirt had stains: ketchup, by the looks of it. Her brown hair was arranged in tangled braids that were almost completely undone, with pieces of her hair sticking up about her head like they had somewhere else to be. Plus, she smelled bad. Well, he couldn't actually smell her, but he was pretty sure that she'd smell like bird poop if he got close enough to get a whiff.

Also, she was floating three feet off the ground.

Jimmy Joe picked up his bat and took a step away from her. "Leave me alone, Piper McCloud."

"Suit yourself." Piper shrugged, then floated away and touched down on the steps of Jameson's store. Jimmy Joe watched her take out a couple of sheets of paper. At the Community Notice Board she relocated a MASSEY FERGUSON TRACTOR FOR SALE from the center and placed her notice in the prime spot.

Jimmy Joe was careful to keep a safe distance.

There was an unwritten law in Lowland County not to go near Piper McCloud. She was strange—dangerous, even—and it could be catching. There was a very good reason why folks said this:

Piper McCloud could fly.

Piper's parents, Betty and Joe McCloud, had tried to hide her when she was small, but the older she got, the more difficult it was to hide a girl who liked to fly. For a while Piper was sent away to a special school that was supposed to fix her, but, as far as anyone could tell, it only made things worse. Not only that, but when she returned from the school, she brought home with her a pack of friends, each one stranger than the next, and the whole passel of them holed up at the McCloud farm, where they were up to untold mischief, or so the good folk in Lowland County thought. They didn't even have the decency to pretend to be normal anymore. Jimmy Joe's mother, Millie Mae, in particular, was affronted by their disturbing behavior.

"It's not right. It ain't the way of things, and they know it," Millie Mae would flap. "You mark my words, Jimmy Joe: no good will come of them kids. They're wicked, and the stars above has their eyes on them."

As Jimmy Joe watched Piper at the notice board, he

could see no sign of her wickedness, only her ineptitude. She was dropping tacks willy-nilly, trying to pick them up and keep the notice on the board all at the same time. She might be able to fly, but she sure as heck couldn't tack a piece of paper up on a board.

Watching her made Jimmy Joe feel antsy and superior. "You gotta hold 'em at an angle," he called out. "Don't drive 'em in straight like that or they won't go."

She took his advice, but her tack tumbled off again.

"Shoot." Jimmy Joe threw his bat down. "Get outta the way! If I don't do it, it'll never get done."

Snatching the tacks out of Piper's hand, he pushed her aside and set about jamming one tack into each corner of the flyer. When he was finished, he stood back to take a look at his work, and it was only then that he read the words on the paper itself.

Flying Lessons
Have you ever wanted to fly?

Now is your chance.

I can teach anyone to fly.

I have years of flying experience.

Beginners welcome!

Contact PIPER McCLOUD

Jimmy Joe felt tricked. "What's this?"

"Flying lessons!" Piper said brightly. "I'll start out with lessons, but maybe in time I can have a whole flying school!"

"No one wants your fool lessons." He snatched up his bat and walked away. "No one cares anything about flying."

"Sure they care!" Piper followed him, bubbling with excitement. "Who wouldn't want to fly? You can get places faster and see things from up high that you can't see when you're on the ground. When the breeze is blowing, it lifts you up, up, up."

There she went with all her talking. Jimmy Joe knew better than to listen, and he waved her away like she was a gnat. Or something lower than a gnat. "That's not true. You don't know what you're saying."

Piper flew over him and landed in front. He made sure not to slow down and that forced her to fly backward.

"I'll tell you this," she said. "One time I was flying over the Grand Canyon, and this condor with wings bigger than my whole body came flying up to me." She spread her arms out wide, causing Jimmy Joe to get a vivid image in his mind's eye of the bird and what it must be like to fly through the Grand Canyon.

"That condor wanted to get a good look at me, so I let 'em. That's the truth. Another time, when I was flying over the Pacific Ocean, I saw something swimming way down low, and it was big and long, but it wasn't a whale. It was something else. Something no one has ever seen before."

"Like what?"

"I dunno."

"What it look like?"

Piper checked to make sure no one was listening, and then she leaned in. "It looked like a sea monster."

Jimmy Joe snorted and pushed her out of the way. "Stop making things up."

"I could teach you flying tricks. I know lots of those."

A fully formed picture of himself diving through the air exploded like a kernel of popcorn inside Jimmy Joe's head, and suddenly his heart began to beat faster. Maybe he'd look good flying. "What kind of tricks?"

Piper threw her arms up. "All kinds. Whatever you want. I learned how to do this corkscrew that turns into a dive. It makes you dizzy, but it's fun all the same."

Those blue eyes of hers were sparkling now in the way she made them shine so that you couldn't look away.

"Or, if you don't want to go high, I can teach you to stay low to the ground and thread through trees. It's tricky, and you gotta be real agile and keep your eyes open." She took his arm, pulling him. "C'mon, we can start your first lesson right now!"

She was so close that her scent went right up his nostrils before he could stop it, but it wasn't like he'd thought; she didn't smell like bird poop or dirt or anything close to that. She smelled like getting a day off school when you weren't expecting to. She smelled like catching a fly ball in your baseball mitt while everyone was watching and cheering. Her smell made him want to hit something.

"I don't want your fool lessons, and no one else will, neither. Get away. Git!"

He pointed his finger at the ground like she was a mangy dog.

"That's not nice," she said. "I was trying to be nice." Her feet dropped down, hitting the dirt in the same sad way a balloon sinks a few days after a birthday party's over. "You see, I got to thinking—wouldn't it be something if I could get other folks to fly. That's what I thought. When I'm flying up in the sky, it feels like pure freedom with a helping of happiness on top. I'm telling you there's nothing else like it. I'd like other folks to know that feeling too, because . . . well"—Piper put her hand on her middle and pressed down against it—"to live your whole life and never know the joy of flying is about the saddest thing I can think of. Wouldn't you like to know what flying feels like too?"

For a moment, Piper's words mesmerized Jimmy Joe, and he found himself nodding. He would like to know that, and so much more besides, but then what would his brothers think? Or his mother? Piper could talk and talk and talk and never stop. If he listened to her for one second more, he was going to do something—something bad. He turned his back to her, but she kept at it.

"I'll teach you for free," she said. "It won't cost you nothing."

"If it don't cost nothing, then it's not worth nothing."

Jimmy Joe started to hit the ground with his bat. Not light taps but violent, mean whacks, like he was hacking off his arm to get out of a trap before a bear ate him.

"I DO NOT . . ."

Whack.

"WANT YOUR LESSONS . . ."

Whack. Whack.

"LEAVE ME BE!"

Whack. Whack. Whack.

That shut her piehole. Piper stood watching him and his bat with a curious expression on her face. Almost like she was thinking that he was the one who was strange.

He kept at it for a while, but it was tiring hitting the ground with a baseball bat, and it made his arm hurt, so he stopped. Now he was panting and sweaty and hot, and it was all her fault.

Apparently, she couldn't care less how he was feeling and instead had taken to gazing off at something in the distance. He caught sight of a swirl of dust approaching at an impossible speed. Fast like a tornado. It was coming right at them.

Jimmy Joe froze. Should he run? Duck? What in the heck could this thing be? It swerved sharply around a tree, turned the corner by Doc Bell's office, and blazed a path right at their hearts. It was coming so fast there was no time to think.

Then the swirl came up to Piper and stopped dead in front of her. The dust blew into Jimmy Joe's face and wafted straight into his lungs. Before he had a chance to hack it out, he discovered that the swirl had turned into a girl; or, he realized, she wasn't a swirl, but she'd been running so fast she had created one. Now she was standing right in front of Piper McCloud like it was the most natural thing in the world.

"Conrad wants you," said the girl to Piper. She was tall, a beanpole with shaggy dark hair covering half her face. She was older than they were; Jimmy Joe guessed fifteen.

"Tell Conrad I'm busy right now, Myrtle." Piper jammed her box of tacks into her pocket.

"Conrad says it's urgent." The girl, Myrtle, shot a glance Jimmy Joe's way. She flicked her head in his direction. "Who's that?"

"That's Jimmy Joe Miller."

Myrtle kept looking at him like she had the right to look and not be polite. Like he was an animal in the zoo, and she'd bought a ticket and could stare for as long as she wanted. "Who?"

"They've got the farm next to ours," Piper said significantly.

"You mean he's a *local*?" Myrtle rolled her eyes and turned away; it was time to move on.

Jimmy Joe could feel his fist tighten around the bat. Who did that girl think she was, treating him as though he wasn't worth the time of day?

"Conrad says we have to move out right away."

Piper looked up the street to the notice board on the side of the church. "But I've got to post a few more signs . . ."

Myrtle's eyebrow shot up to her hairline. "Max is at it again."

"Max? Again?" Piper sagged. "Darn it."

Jimmy Joe was standing right there, and they were talking like he didn't exist. He should walk away and ignore them as they were ignoring him. But he was interested. What were these kids up to? Everyone in Lowland County would be dying to know. "Who's Max?" he said.

"None of your beeswax." Myrtle kept her attention

on Piper. "Conrad told me to tell you"—she cleared her throat and lowered her voice—"'Piper, in case it's slipped your mind, there's a madman trying to destroy this world, and the only thing that stands between him and total chaos is us. So get back here, because you know we can't do it without you.'" Myrtle put her hand to her throat and cleared it again.

"Conrad doesn't sound like that," Piper said, and blew frustration out of her mouth and nose. "Fine. Tell Conrad I'm on my way."

Myrtle threw off a mock salute and disappeared. Or appeared to disappear. She ran so fast that one moment she was there, and the next a cloud of dust was whipping past Jimmy Joe, covering him for a second time. Jimmy Joe coughed and wiped dirt off his tongue with the back of his hand. What he wouldn't give to run like that. If he could run fast, he'd be faster than that Myrtle, and then he'd leave *her* in a cloud of dust, and she could see how she liked it.

Piper folded up her flyers and jammed them in her pocket along with the tacks. Then she began to float.

The sight of her feet dangling in midair hit Jimmy Joe's gut. "We don't want you here. G'on home," he spat.

"How would you know if you want me or not? You don't know me."

"I know all I need to know."

"You know what, Jimmy Joe?" Her hackles were up, and it was making her face flush pink. "I bet you would have been a good flier if you'd given it a chance. But now you'll never know, 'cause you're too scared to try. Like a *'fraidy-cat*."

Jimmy Joe's back snapped straight. "I'm no 'fraidy-cat."

"Oh yeah?"

Throwing one arm up above her head, Piper rocketed into the air. In a matter of seconds she was so high she didn't look like more than a dot in the sky. Then she came down, down, down—gunning for Jimmy Joe.

What kind of outrageous things would an outrageous girl like her do? Jimmy Joe didn't know, and he didn't want to find out. He dropped to the dirt, throwing his arms over his head. She swooped down on him so close, the air above his ear felt the tickle of her not more than a paper's slice away—that's how close she came to him.

"'Fraidy-cat," she called out, flying away and not coming back.

That was the final straw: Jimmy Joe jumped to his feet and ran to the bulletin board. He ripped Piper McCloud's notice off the board, sending tacks flying in all directions. He crumpled the paper up and jammed it into his pocket.

"Let's see how many flying students you get now, Piper McCloud!" he called out, waving his fist in the air. Piper didn't turn, probably couldn't even hear him, she was up so high.

Jimmy Joe stood in the middle of the empty street, his bat in one hand, his fist in the air. Darn Piper McCloud and her flying. And darn those others she was with too and all the fancy things they were probably getting up to at that very moment.

The horsefly came back, buzzing around his head, but Jimmy Joe didn't bother to swing at it. He'd lost all hope of finding someone to play ball with, let alone getting the chance to beat them. There was nothing for him to do and no one to do it with, and he might as well just go home. Allowing his bat to sag to the ground, he turned toward the Miller farm, walking slowly in the heat.

CHAPTER

2

*P*IPER FLEW LIKE AN ARROW. SHE KEPT her arms close to her body, her legs straight, and her toes pointed. It was nothing for her to fly from Main Street to the McCloud farm, a couple of measly miles, less than a minute of her time.

The sky was dotted with cumulus clouds, and Piper sliced through them, getting a cool misting on an unseasonably hot day. Below, the fields were turned over and ready for planting; spring had come to Lowland County.

There wasn't much to Lowland County. It was tucked up in the "pay it no mind" part of the country and consisted of forty-five assorted farms, painstakingly planted and tilled by the sweat of generations. Nothing in particular ever happened in Lowland County, and that's the way the people there liked it. Folks got born, grew up, worked the land, went to church on Sunday, kept a keen eye on their neighbor's business, and, in the fullness of time and without too much fuss, passed on to the promised land. That was the way of things.

The McCloud farm was stuck smack-dab in the middle of Lowland County, and for generations the McClouds had done exactly as they were supposed to in the order they were supposed to do it. All of that changed the day Piper was born, and it changed even more when she brought her friends to live at the farm. Since the arrival of the brood of exceptional children, the McCloud farm had been transformed from struggling to prosperous. Acres of neatly planted crops, a herd of cattle, a healthy flock of sheep, and a teeming chicken coop were situated around a big old barn, tractor sheds, newly installed cow barns, and the little white clapboard house, which sported freshly painted blue shutters and flowered window boxes.

It was the old barn that Piper flew toward, like a homing pigeon returning to the roost. From the outside it appeared to be no different from any other barn in Lowland County. In truth, it was the base of operations for the most sophisticated and unusual bunch of kids in the world.

Piper touched down in the farmyard and went for the barn door that had been rigged to scan the DNA of anyone who tried to enter. It quickly identified Piper, and she stepped into a world that was equal parts futuristic science lab and crime-fighting headquarters, all in the confines of a rickety old barn.

Piper did not stop to marvel at the monitors with multiple satellite feeds, contraptions that were both highly advanced and strangely constructed; she didn't have time to look at the individual work areas positioned around the perimeter of the barn, each one as different as the ability of the kid who occupied it. Above her in the loft was a laboratory, and she could hear strange experiments in the works that Conrad had bubbling and brewing. Photographs had begun to gather on the walls, evidence of the adventures they'd had, the places they'd been, and the people they'd met. Nor did she stop to take a metal clamp out of Fido's mouth. Fido was Conrad's pet, a strange combination of lizard, bat, and dog. He'd recently developed a nasty habit of stealing important things and chewing them into something else entirely.

Instead, Piper strode to the center of the organized chaos, where a team-meeting table stood. Seated around the table waiting for her were ten children who ranged from nine to seventeen years old. Over the last couple of years, this group of kids had not only lived together, but worked together and grown up together. This had transformed them into the strongest of teams and the closest of families.

At the head of the table stood fourteen-year-old Conrad, who was the brains of the operation—as was befitting a super genius—and the mastermind behind the transformation of the McClouds' barn into a high-tech haven. He was, in action and deed, neat and precise, like a walking fact. He was also Piper's best friend.

Sitting next to Conrad were twin boys Nalen and Ahmed Mustafa, lolling back in their chairs and randomly poking at each other or, if they could get away with it, sending a spitball down the table to an unsuspecting victim. Even though Nalen and Ahmed were the oldest of the group, having passed their seventeenth birthday, they were the most likely to cause mischief. Conrad was always careful to keep a sharp eye on them, because there was no telling what two boys with the ability to change the weather from a sunny day to a blizzard in the blink of an eye could get up to.

Next to the twins sat Jasper and Violet, the most quiet and timid of the group. Jasper had just reached his ninth birthday and, for the most part, had outgrown his nervous stutter. He was a delicate waif of a boy who possessed a wondrous ability to heal and whose deep empathy was matched only by Violet. Violet was currently half her normal size, as she'd just been hit on the side of the head by Nalen's spitball. She startled easily and could shrink to a remarkably small size, either by her own design or when afraid. When she was at her normal size, Violet was a shy beauty, with her dark complexion and soulful brown eyes. Despite her retiring nature, Violet was a much valued and loved member of the group for her loyalty and her quiet courage.

"We have a lot to cover this morning," Conrad said, pulling the attention of the group to him. He'd isolated the place on the electronic globe that he was looking for and was ready to start the meeting. "I need your full attention. As you know, my family, along with Dr. Hellion and J., sent word this morning that they were entering Xanthia." Conrad showed their position in a mountainous region on the map. "The Chosen Ones have severed communication with us, and my father's goal is to make contact with them and ascertain their status. He will get word to us as soon as he can."

Satisfied that this information had been absorbed, Conrad swiped the image away and pulled up a windswept beach in the Caribbean and another item on his agenda. "Next—I came across this disaster area. Would anyone here care to explain it?"

Ahmed and Nalen groaned at the same time and slumped down in their seats. "It's not what you think," Nalen said.

Ahmed agreed. "We didn't do anything."

"And yet," Conrad said, "destruction seems to follow. According to my calculations, it is highly improbable that a tropical storm would erupt unexpectedly, hit one beach only, and then dissipate all within the course of ninety minutes. The same ninety minutes, I might add, that you happened to be surfing on that beach."

"Who can predict the weather?" Nalen shrugged.

"Someone who can change the weather," Conrad retorted.

Ahmed put his hands over his head. "You're picking on us."

"Piper's here!" Smitty interrupted, catching sight of her heading for the table. Smitty had X-ray vision, so he usually spotted things before anyone else. Now sixteen, Smitty had recently shed his braces and grown the beginnings of biceps, and each day he took great pains to carefully comb back his hair, all for the benefit of Kimber. Even though Kimber sat directly across the table from Smitty, she noticed none of these things; Kimber was not a romantic or lovestruck sort of girl. Kimber was the sort of girl who could tase a boy, and often did, with the vast voltage of electricity in her fingertips. Romance made Kimber feel squeamish, and she shielded her growing body with baggy clothes. Seeing Piper approach, Kimber threw the ball of static electricity that she'd been playing with in her hands.

"Hey, Piper. Think fast!"

Piper easily dodged it and plopped down at her seat on the far side of the table, facing Conrad.

"I held off on the important stuff until you got here," Conrad said to her before turning back to Ahmed and pointing at the beach. "What did I tell you the last time this happened?"

"We were only surfing." Ahmed slouched. "Since when is surfing a crime?"

"Since you created a windstorm that did this." Conrad gazed at the damage to the beach.

"It wasn't our fault." Nalen planted his elbows on the table. "You can't convict us without proof."

"Oh, you want proof?" Conrad quickly accessed satellite information and began displaying it for the twins, who began to refute it and find fault with it.

From experience, Piper knew that this entire argument could take time, so she leaned back in her chair and turned to Lily Yakimoto, who had the seat to her right.

"What'd I miss?" Piper whispered to Lily.

"Max is up to something." Lily kept her voice low. "But Conrad didn't want to go into details until you got here. Something about a big attack and world danger and, you know, the usual."

"Not more orphans, I hope," Piper said. "Max has been doing that a lot lately."

"I know, right?" Lily telekinetically pulled a pen off her workstation on the other side of the barn. The pen zipped across, made a sharp detour around Daisy, and landed in Lily's hand. She quickly applied it to the pad of paper in front of her.

Glancing over, Piper caught sight of Lily's page. Besides being telekinetic, Lily was a budding dress designer and had a passion for fashion. Like Jasper, Lily was nine years old, but despite her youth, she had the poise and fashion sense of a young Coco Chanel.

"Nice!" Piper whispered, admiring her sketch. "What's that for?"

"The spring dance," Lily whispered back.

Piper was all ears. "You're going to the spring dance?"

"*Everyone's* going to the dance," Lily said with authority. "Aren't you?"

Piper swallowed. "I dunno."

WHEN THE LOWLAND COUNTY SPRING DANCE had been announced at church the Sunday before, Piper had realized that she had two pressing problems: she didn't have a dress that fit, and, in order to attend the dance, someone would first have to ask her.

The moment church let out, Piper flew home ahead of the others to discuss her predicament with her mother.

"I can't go to the dance if I don't have a dress, but I've grown two inches since Christmas, and now they're all too short. My blue cotton's so plain." Piper clutched her hands together and started to float. "Jameson's store got some new dresses in the window. Maybe I could try one on?"

Betty McCloud was a round, plain woman, and she sniffed at the notion of store-bought clothes. "I'll take a look at your blue cotton and see if I can't let it down. No cause to go buying things we don't need; waste not, want not, I always say."

"But, Ma, I'm twelve years old! I can't wear a dress meant for babies."

"Twelve is still a youngen through and through. Besides, I'm not sure a child your age is ready to go off to a dance."

"But I'm not a child anymore, and *everyone* will be there. I *have* to go!"

"And if everyone jumped off a cliff, I suppose you'd jump too," Betty replied tartly.

"I jump off cliffs all the time!"

"Don't sass me, child."

"But—"

Betty's hand flew into the air before Piper's argument could become airborne. "I mean what I say, Piper. Not another word."

PIPER SHIFTED IN HER SEAT AND THREADED her fingers together. "I can't go to the dance, Lily. I don't have anything to wear."

Lily sighed as though she were dealing with a child who was much, much younger. "Obvi," she said. "Like I didn't know that!" Flipping the pages on her pad, she came to another design and revealed it to Piper.

"Wow! That's something." The dress was simple with a full skirt, feminine but not frothy. It was Piper's dream of a dress. "It's beautiful!"

"I know." Lily did not suffer from pangs of modesty and saw no need to pretend she did. "I already made it. It's yours." Pulling the page free, she handed it to Piper. "Problem solved."

Piper clutched the paper dress before turning it over discretely on the table. "I . . . uh . . . I don't know. It's probably not a good idea that I go to the dance. I think I'll stay home."

Lily was affronted. "You can't stay home. We're all going. Everyone will be there. The dress is ready!"

An embarrassed heat burned Piper's complexion. Lily's eyes narrowed as she rooted into the crux of the issue. "Wait a second," she said. "Did someone ask you to the dance?"

Piper's face went from pink to red. "Pffff." She puffed like it was a stupid question, like the answer was obvious. Then she turned back to Lily. "Did someone ask you?"

"Jasper asked me," Lily said quickly. "I had to tell him to ask me, but as soon as I told him to, he did. When I overcame my surprise and natural feminine shyness at his bold request, I, of course, agreed to accompany him. Smitty asked Kimber. Daisy and Myrtle are going as friends. Ahmed and Nalen are going too, but they won't tell me who they're going with." Lily rolled her eyes. "Probably no one. Violet says she'd shrink too much and wants to stay home." Lily took a deep breath after this report and then bit on her pencil as she considered Piper's predicament. "So who asked you?"

Piper swallowed, her eyes falling to her lap. "No one asked me."

Lily tsked over this news. "This won't do," she whispered. She wasn't going to have this for one second; she'd designed the dress, she'd decided they were all going, and Piper was ruining her plans. "Conrad will ask you to the dance," she decided.

Piper's face turned into an inferno of heat. "Conrad's my best friend. I'm not going to a dance with him."

"Conrad likes you," Lily pointed out.

"Yes, because we're friends."

"No, he *likes* you." Lily tried this idea on for size, and it suited the situation nicely. Now that it was decided, she took it one step further. "He probably loves you."

"What?" Piper squeaked loudly.

Conrad turned from his rendering model and looked at Piper. "I said we need to communicate our positions to each other as we're moving," Conrad repeated. Suddenly he noticed the extreme color of Piper's face. "Piper? Are you sick?"

"N–no," Piper stuttered.

"She needs a glass of water," Lily said, taking command of the situation. "Come on, Piper." Grabbing Piper's arm, Lily led her away.

"The reason Conrad hasn't asked you is because of this," Lily continued when they were out of earshot, pointing her pencil at Piper's head, and then up and down her body.

"This?" Piper looked herself over. "What?"

"You! You are the problem." Lily grabbed one of the bands off Piper's braids, freeing her hair. "Boys like it when your hair is loose and curly."

"They do?"

"Of course they do. And you should flip it around a bit too; it catches their attention." Lily flipped her shining hair to demonstrate.

Piper flipped her hair, but it tangled about in messy clumps.

"And this!" Lily pulled at Piper's old T-shirt and jeans. "You can't wear this!"

"But this is my favorite T-shirt, and these jeans are so comfortable." Piper wrapped her arms around herself to protect her favorite clothes.

Lily shook her head like she was dealing with a disobedient child and handed Piper a glass of water. "Dresses are more feminine. Look at me." Lily turned around, allowing Piper to admire her lovely silk dress. "This is how you should look. If you want Conrad to ask you to the dance, you need to look like me."

"But I'm not trying to get Conrad to ask me to the dance!" Piper was flustered beyond belief.

"But you want to go to the dance, right?"

Piper did want to go. She did want to wear the nice dress that Lily had made for her, and she did want someone to ask her. But after that it got complicated. She wasn't sure how it would feel to dance with a boy, and she wasn't sure she wanted to do that. Everything suddenly felt different than it had before.

"I want to go the dance," she admitted.

Lily held up a single finger. "Not another word. I will take care of everything."

THREE HOURS LATER, LILY PRESENTED PIPER to herself in front of a full-length mirror.

The image that Piper saw belonged to someone else entirely. Her hair had been turned into a waterfall of golden-brown waves cascading over her shoulders. A cheeky curl over her left eye completed her coif. Lily had applied a sheer pink lip gloss on Piper's lips, and it sparkled when it caught the light. Piper's dress fit her to perfection—elegant and sweet, folds of blue silk dotted with pearls around the waist and bodice.

"Golly," Piper breathed. "I don't recognize myself."

"Exactly!" Lily crossed her arms over her chest, satisfied with her work. "From now on this is how you are going to look all the time. Mark my words: Conrad will be on his knee begging you to go to the dance in less than twenty-four hours, or my name isn't Lily Yakimoto."

Lily slid a golden flower hair clip in the shape of a lily (what else?) out of her hair and fixed it on Piper's head. "There. Now you're perfect!"

The hair clip was heavy and substantial; Piper felt the weight of it pressing down on her skull. As she turned her head, the clip twinkled.

"You're practically a grown-up." Lily said. "If you want to get invited to a dance and be a grown-up, you've got to be less . . ." Lily looked at Piper, and her hands fluttered as she attempted to capture just the right word to encapsulate her feelings. "You have to be less you and more *this*."

"*This?*"

"Yes. This!" Lily waved her hands up and down Piper's coiffed and perfectly outfitted form. "This is grown-up. This is you!"

"Oh." Piper looked at the "you" in the mirror. She did look fabulous; there was no denying that. She looked like a young lady. But still . . . she felt awkward and strange and uncomfortable and definitely not herself. She felt heavy. "I guess I'm not used to it yet. But that'll just take time, right?"

A gust of wind announced the arrival of Myrtle, who was suddenly standing right in front of them. "We're moving out in sixty minutes," she started to say before she caught a glimpse of Piper and did a double take. "What's wrong with you? Is it Halloween and I forgot?"

Piper shrunk back, embarrassed. "Oh, it's nothing . . ."

"You look so . . . so . . ."

"Elegant? Grown-up?" Lily offered.

"Weird," Myrtle said decisively.

"You only think she looks weird because you have

the fashion sense of a garbage collector," Lily retorted. "Piper looks like a young lady!"

"Uh. Whatever." Clearly, Myrtle didn't think so. "Conrad wanted to make sure that Piper is ready to move out."

Lily lifted her eyebrow and gave Piper a significant look. "Conrad *wants* Piper?"

Myrtle's face screwed up. "Conrad wants *all of us*. We've got to go! You guys are acting odd. I'm out of here." Myrtle zipped away.

"Mark my words." Lily smiled smugly. "Something big is about to happen to you, Piper McCloud."

CHAPTER

3

"IT'S A GOOD DAY FOR IT," MAX SAID TO himself.

Max had a habit of talking to himself. It was, he thought, an occupational hazard of living forever; the only person you have to speak with consistently over the years is yourself. It was a good thing Max was the most interesting, most likable person he knew.

"I'm a great guy," Max often said. "I'm lucky to have myself."

Max had boyish good looks, a charming smile, and tousled blond hair. Anyone who looked at him would guess his age to be sixteen. He encouraged this impression by wearing jeans, high-tops, and a black T-shirt with the words CHILLIN' LIKE A VILLAIN across the front.

Max was not subtle. And he was not sixteen.

Max had positioned a mesh sports chair so that he had a prime view. Settling in, he pulled a cold soda out of his backpack and slid it into the handy cupholder.

Genius, these cupholders! Why had it taken so long for them to be invented? The Romans would have gone bananas for a decent cupholder in their chariots.

Max knew that Conrad and Piper knew he was up to something. He knew they knew that he knew this. He also knew they would be getting into position all around him at that very moment. He'd grant them a few minutes more to ready themselves; he was a generous guy. Plus, he hated to rush things.

Oh, this was going to be fun!

Did he have the best angle? Through the waning darkness, the large stones of Stonehenge loomed in front of him. They stood now, just as they had for the last five thousand years, mysterious and tall.

Esteemed archeologists and scientists had long circled the stones, scratching their heads and guessing at what could have possessed farmers to drag them into a field in the middle of nowhere. The work, they'd say, the impossibility of dragging massive stones from mines that were over one hundred miles away without decent equipment, was unthinkable.

And yet it had happened, and the stones stood

through wars and famines and plagues and all that came and went as time passed.

But why? What purpose did the stones serve? Perhaps they were the location of a religious rite or a lost church, it was surmised. Maybe they were a giant sundial set up to track the movement of the sun. No one could say for sure.

No one but Max, that is. Because Max had been alive then and had seen it all clearly, remembered what everyone else has long forgotten: how the farmers stopped fighting each other, put aside their petty squabbles and their fear of starvation, left their fields, and worked side by side to erect the stones with exacting precision.

Max remembered, like it was yesterday, standing in the mud and rain, watching those farmers battling for their lives. He knew they would have dragged stones from thousands of miles away if that's what it took.

Because the very lives of their children depended on it.

Because the truth is that Stonehenge is not a church or a calendar or even a gathering place: Stonehenge is a prison. As long as the stones stand, the ancient beasts trapped beneath sleep. Max knew all about the beasts and what would happen if they were released.

Which is why that day was a day for the history books.

"I'm not saying it wasn't fun," Max mused to himself, considering the last year, in which he'd embraced the role of villain. At every turn he'd caused trouble and watched the kids figure out how to stop him. "The kids are good, and Conrad's smart: a worthy adversary. I haven't had that before, and it has made life interesting to have something to fight against."

"Agreed," Max responded to himself. He was the most agreeable person he knew. It made talking to himself such a joy. "But you can only play a villain for so long before it becomes . . . repetitive and boring."

The very mention of the words "boring" and "repetitive" made Max shudder. To successfully live forever, Max had some very strict rules. He called them the Rules of Fun, and he followed them religiously.

Max's Rules of Fun for Living Forever

- Always have your next fun thing planned. (Keep moving, set goals, always move toward fun.)
- Never repeat yourself. (Repetition leads to boredom. Repetition kills fun.)
- Avoid all unfun. (Anything that can die is a buzzkill. Stay away from it at all costs.)

Playing "world disaster" with Piper and Conrad had been fun. No doubt. But still . . . boredom and repetition must be avoided at all costs.

"No rules were broken," Max said firmly. "We strapped that bus of orphans on the bridge, but a few months before, it was a boatload of orphans going over a waterfall. There were similarities."

Max shoved some chips into his mouth, chewing angrily. "One set of orphans was from the inner city and the other set was foreign born. That is very, very different."

"It was on the line. Plus they were both easily rescued by Piper and Conrad's team of wonder kids. It wasn't even that fun."

Max smushed up the bag and littered fitfully. "I have never ever broken the rules, and you know that." *Why must he be such a nitpicker? And on a night like this, too!*

"Just saying . . ."

"And I'm saying that we've agreed it's over now and we aren't going to play games with the kids anymore, so why do we need to keep talking about it? Today will finish it. Why do you have to go and ruin it?"

Max hated it when he got like this. He was the most exasperating person he knew. And the worst part of it was that he couldn't get away from himself.

He chugged back the rest of his soda, crumpled up the can, and tossed it over his shoulder, slouching into his chair peevishly. Maybe he'd give himself the silent treatment for a bit. A time-out wouldn't hurt.

"It is a very good plan," he admitted begrudgingly out of the side of his mouth.

"Of course it's a good plan. It's the best plan. Inventive. Interesting. And fun."

"Yes, it will be fun."

Uncomfortable pause.

"I'm sorry."

"No, I'm sorry."

"Let's just forget about it."

"It's forgotten. You're a great guy, Max!"

"Thanks, Max."

Max sighed, relieved. Nothing should ruin a day like this. Adjusting his position so that he was exactly as he wanted to be, he plucked the detonator out of the other cupholder.

"Okay, Max, this is it. Are you ready?"

"I was born ready." Max pumped his fist in the air. "This is a Max Attack!"

Max gleefully pressed the detonator's button. On cue, the bombs he'd tucked beneath the stones exploded, earth and fire shooting outward.

The force of the explosions shifted the ground, and one by one the monolithic stones tumbled, some shattering to pieces, others falling with a thud. The biggest stone fell against the ones closest to it and took them down like dominoes. At last only one single solitary stone remained. It wobbled, leaning right and left.

"C'mon, baby," Max cheered. "Come to Papa."

The stone teetered.

Max became aware of a flash of movement circling the destruction. The kids were familiar sights to Max now; he could anticipate their moves, which was another reason it was time to stop playing with them.

"That must be Myrtle," he said. "Probably running the perimeter for a closer look." Something caught his eye above the site. "And there's Piper McCloud, circling for an overhead view of things. Right on schedule."

He placed his index finger in the air. "Cue a thunderstorm."

Sure enough, storm clouds were brewing overhead, courtesy of the weather-changing wonders, Ahmed and Nalen Mustafa.

"Yes, having a rainstorm on standby in case of a fire is good thinking, Conrad," Max agreed.

In a painful, slow-motion way, the last stone leaned to the right and then the left and then back again.

"Ahhhh," said Max, gleefully clutching himself. "The suspense is killing me."

Slowly the final rock of Stonehenge fell to the ground. The impact of the stone's fall was felt for miles around.

"Touchdown!" Max stood up, his arms raised above his head.

Silence.

Then came a rumble. The earth began to shake gently, like it had a stomachache and was about to belch. The shaking grew.

CRACK! A nasty fissure split the soil down the middle of where the stones had once stood. Out of the wound oozed a black, hairy bug the size of a boulder.

The bug was the thing of nightmares. There was slime on it and spiky hair sticking out of its many legs. It was midnight black, only made possible by the complete absence of goodness and light. It stood, directing its many antenna about and shaking off crusted dirt. Next, it flexed its wings and lifted its head, opening a vast mouth to roar.

Max covered his ears.

Then the bug took flight and went directly up, up, up.

The earth it left behind was now bubbling and shaking and falling inward. Out came another bug, identical to the one that had flown away. A moment later came another, and now there was a seemingly endless stream of them, arriving and shaking and then flying away.

The hole was growing, swallowing the earth around it.

"Ahhhhhh," came a scream.

Max grabbed the pair of night-vision binoculars in his bag. (He was nothing if not prepared.) He scanned the area until he found what he was looking for—a kid in the middle of the chaos.

"That looks like Jasper," Max reported to himself. Jasper was a gentle, stuttering thing that Max never paid much mind to since there was little fun in him, at least inasmuch as Max discerned fun.

"Hmmm. A child in danger definitely takes the stakes up a notch." Max smacked his lips together.

Jasper clung to the side of the crater, holding on for dear life. The mound shook and shuddered, bits falling away. Jasper was not large for his age, and the violent shaking of the earth was tossing his small body about like a piece of popcorn.

And then Jasper lost his hold.

He slipped into the crater and out of sight.

Max sat back, irritated by the short-term nature of this particular plot twist. "Well, that didn't last long," he said, throwing up his hands like he'd gone to an unsatisfactory movie and deserved his money back.

But then—happiness! A sudden flash of movement swooped down into the crater after Jasper.

"Piper to the rescue!" Max cheered, watching and waiting for Piper to reappear.

Long moments passed, but Piper was nowhere to be seen. "The plot thickens," Max said ominously, delighted. "Will Piper McCloud meet a nasty end? Or will she save her fallen comrade and return victorious?"

More and more bugs were pouring out of the hungry mouth of the crater. Overhead, storm clouds swirled into an angry soup, throwing off bolts of lightning and hearty thunder.

Still no sign of Piper.

"I'm on the edge of my seat," Max chortled. And he was. He was leaning forward, perched at the ready, night-vision goggles jammed to his face. "There's no way that Piper McCloud will ever get out of this jam."

But then . . . Piper flew up! Debris pelted her from all sides. Drama and pain on her face, Jasper an unconscious rag doll in her arms.

When she cleared the edge of the crater, Piper tumbled out of the air and down to the ground, landing in a heap. Jasper a second heap next to her.

And then . . . a bug came crawling up out of the crater right at the two of them.

If Piper had remained still—like Jasper, who was unconscious—she would have been safe, but she kicked at the bug and struggled. The instinctive response of the bug was to attack.

The belly of the bug ignited into an angry red burn, and then it stung her. Piper's body bucked and shook. After that, she was absolutely still.

"Unbelievable!" Max clapped his hands together, entirely satisfied. "The perfect ending!"

CHAPTER

4

$\mathcal{I}$T WAS LATE IN THE AFTERNOON WHEN
Betty returned to the farm from her ladies' sewing
circle to find Piper unconscious on the kitchen table,
surrounded on all sides by the anxious faces of the other
kids. They were all, without exception, slathered in
muck, debris, and panic.

"Lord above!" Betty dropped her basket and put her
hand over her heart. "What in heaven's name is going
on here?"

Conrad was carefully turning Piper over with the
help of Daisy's strong hands. "Max set a trap, and Piper
got caught in it. She was stung by a bug, and by the time
I reached her, she wasn't breathing."

"She ain't breathing?" Betty kept her eyes on Piper's
white face and blue lips.

"She's breathing now," Kimber said quickly. "I
helped with that. I gave her a good jolt."

Kimber clapped her hands together, and a blue arch of fizzling electricity crackled between them. When she was younger, Kimber used to have accidents, blow things up, short out entire electrical grids, but that didn't happen anymore.

"I pumped a thousand volts into her chest to get her heart started, and as soon as I zapped her, she was breathing again."

The visual this created in Betty's head was anything but comforting.

"Hold her steady," Conrad said to Daisy, who had to concentrate on not crushing Piper with her super strength. Smitty pushed forward, squinting his X-ray vision so that he could get the precise magnification.

"She's got no broken bones," he reported. "No internal bleeding, no trauma to her organs. But hold on—here's the problem."

Smitty pointed to Piper's lower back. "I haven't seen this before."

Conrad unbuttoned the back of Piper's dress, uncovering a red mark the size of a melon on her lower back. In the epicenter of the welt was a wicked puncture wound.

Smitty leaned in close. "When the bug stung, it left behind a type of venom."

"Dear Lord," Betty gasped. "What kind of bug makes a mark like *that*?"

"What are we going to do?" Violet breathed, shrinking several inches. "What if she never wakes up?"

Strained and serious looks passed between the kids.

"Let me try again," said Jasper, coming forward. He was badly shaken up from his time in the crater and had already tried to heal her, but with everything that had gone on, he was having an off day.

Standing back, the kids gave Jasper room to work. Rubbing his hands together, he blew into them until a white light burned brightly inside his flesh. He placed his illuminated hands on Piper, and the light traveled out of him and into her.

Betty said a silent prayer, her lips moving as she watched the light zing inside of Piper's body. Gradually it dissipated and then dimmed altogether. They waited, leaning in slightly and hoping.

A feeble moan drifted out of Piper, so soft and low they all gathered close to make sure they weren't mistaken.

"Piper?" Conrad whispered urgently. "Piper, can you hear me?"

With the utmost care, Daisy turned Piper over and laid her flat.

Suddenly Piper's blue eyes snapped open, her mouth gasping for air like she'd been submerged and had just reached the surface.

Betty near about fainted.

"Oh, Piper, I thought you were dead!" little Violet cried.

Smitty gave Kimber a big hug. (Smitty was always looking for an excuse to hug Kimber, and in the excitement, she let him.)

While the others sagged with relief, Conrad stayed close, watching Piper's confused face for signs.

Piper felt like she was only half there. "What happened, Con? I can't remember."

"You were stung by the bug."

"What bug? Am I alright?" Piper tried to sit up. "I don't feel like myself."

"Rest," Conrad said, a troubled look on his brow. "You need to rest."

In short order Piper was tucked up in her bed with strict instructions to stay put. Betty got busy on a big meal, and Conrad got to work feverishly gathering what information he could on the bugs.

Piper was fussed over to no end; flowers were picked and placed on her bedside table, tasty treats were offered, and every manner of book or amusement was conjured in the hopes it would speed her recovery. When Betty brought up a big bowl of chicken noodle soup and found Piper's room cluttered with kids, she shooed them all away and commanded Piper to rest.

"Do I look okay, Ma?" Piper anxiously balanced her spoon over the large bowl of soup.

To Betty's eyes, Piper looked anything but okay. She was pale, with dark smudges shadowing her eyes, her lips more blue then pink—and there was a tremor in her hand.

"You look like you need a good night's sleep," Betty sniffed. "I don't know how many times I've got to tell you to keep your feet on the ground. Look at the trouble you got yourself into today." Betty still hadn't recovered from the shock of seeing Piper unconscious. "A decent rest will do you a world of good."

Piper nodded hopefully. "And when I wake up in the morning, I'll feel like myself again?"

"You'll be as right as rain," Betty said staunchly.

CHAPTER

5

*P*IPER WOKE FROM TANGLED, MURKY dreams in the small hours of the morning. It was dark inside and out, and there was a heaviness that held her down in her bed. It took considerable strength for Piper to lift her head off the pillow. When she was sitting upright, she looked down at her body, and it felt foreign and suddenly not her own. When had she grown so tall? Her spirit felt lost in the larger landscape.

She swung her legs over the side of the bed so her bare feet touched the braided rug on the floor. Piper looked at her toes and wiggled them, surprised when they responded to her commands.

Piper stood and willed herself to float.

When her feet didn't rise up off the floor, she closed her eyes and tried again. Nothing.

A cold shiver crawled up the base of Piper's neck,

raising goose bumps on the flesh of her arms. She told herself to remain calm and considered what to do.

Get outside. If you can see the sky, you'll naturally go to it.

In the hallway outsider her bedroom, Piper leaned heavily on the walls for support. Her body was strangely stiff, and she felt weak. When she arrived in the kitchen, she sat at the table to gather her resources before making her way out of the house.

Standing in the middle of the farmyard, Piper could see a dusting of gold across the eastern horizon. The sun was about to breach, and she looked to the heavens above.

Up, up. Go up.

Piper raised her arms, tilting her head all the way back until her vision was filled with fading stars. She knew that on a morning like this the sky would taste cold and crisp. She reached for it.

Up. UP!

Piper's feet did not, would not, leave the ground.

Soon after Piper was born, she had floated. Her floating came naturally and completely unbidden at any moment of the night or the day. When she had finally started flying, she had to jump off things to get going. Of course, she hadn't needed to do that in years now. She had taught herself to focus her attention in just the right way so that her body would lift off. If floating was a release, then flying was an explosion of happiness inside her chest.

Fly! I can fly! Fly!

Nothing. Piper resorted to clambering up a barrel and jumping off. She fell to the ground like a stone.

Up onto the flatbed of the truck. *JUMP!*

Thunk to the ground.

Off the top of the fence post. *Jump . . .*

Down again. Fast and hard.

Piper's thoughts came in a frenzy now. *The sky, the sky. Have to get back to the sky.*

She looked for something higher she could climb up onto. Anything. Casting about, her eyes settled on the perfect thing, and without another thought she ran to it.

———◆———

EVERYONE WAS WOKEN BY THE SCREAM—IT was not the sort of sound you could sleep through. It was the kind of scream that came out of a wounded animal that was cornered, terrified, and in pain.

A stampede of feet. Smitty was the first one to spot her.

"She's over here!"

They found her on the ground beside the barn, writhing in pain, her nose bleeding, her arm bent to the side. Without delay, Jasper knelt at her side, rubbed his hands together, and gave her healing. When the pain was released and she could catch her breath again, Piper sat up.

"I fell," she said by way of explanation.

This didn't make sense to anyone. "Fell from what?" "How did you fall?" "What are you talking about? Just fly."

"I've been trying to fly all morning," Piper insisted, getting to her feet. "Watch."

Piper took a step away and looked up, willing herself to the sky. They'd seen her do this same move hundreds, if not thousands, of times. This morning Piper's body didn't move up, and her feet stuck to the ground.

"See? It's not working." Turning around, Piper went to a ladder propped up against the barn and resolutely climbed it. "Now watch this." From the very top of the ladder Piper dove into the air.

As everyone watched, Piper fell down, down, down, landing on the ground with a sickening thud. Once again, there was blood and pain. Once again, Jasper rushed to heal her. When she was whole again, Piper sat up and drew her knees to her chest, hugging them.

"I don't know what to do," Piper said, looking to Lily, to Violet, then to Conrad.

"I feel different too." Piper's hand pressed the place

in her stomach where her deepest feelings lived. "I can't feel the sky inside me."

Each of the kids intimately understood the feeling she was speaking about. Violet's feeling came from wanting to be small and hide; Conrad's feeling was an unquenchable thirst for knowledge; Myrtle's feeling was the need to escape. All of them, without exception, had been born with "the feeling," and to suddenly be bereft of it was . . . unimaginable.

"I can't fly," Piper said. "What am I going to do? I. CAN'T. FLY."

CHAPTER

6

"SHE'S IN SHOCK," SOMEONE SAID WHEN Piper didn't have the strength to stand. Her body had started to tremble uncontrollably, and Conrad had to pick her up and carry her to the barn. Very gently, he placed her in her chair at the team-meeting table.

"Don't worry—I'm going to fix this," Conrad vowed.

"We'll get you back to your normal self in no time." Violet patted Piper's arm.

Without a word everyone sat in their chairs at the table, poised and ready.

"Ideas?" Conrad prompted.

"I can telekinetically get her back into the sky. Maybe when she's up there for long enough, she'll be able to stay up there."

"Why don't we figure out the venom, and Conrad can create a vaccine?"

"Maybe if Jasper healed her again."

"Kimber can shock it out of her, and that'll reboot her system."

"All she needs is some rest."

Conrad pulled up an image of the bug, zooming in on its underbelly.

"I've never seen anything like it," Smitty said.

"It could be a mutation from two different species or DNA that's been genetically modified," Conrad pointed out. "Part cockroach, part virus, part dinosaur."

Nalen snorted. "That would be just like Max to figure out a way to create some sort of superbug bent on world destruction."

"Like a cyber bug," Ahmed agreed.

Conrad tilted his head, considering everything. "We need more information," he decided. "Smitty, Jasper, and Kimber, I want you to isolate and pull out samples of the venom still inside Piper. Myrtle, Daisy, and the twins, you're going to figure out how to predict if and where more bugs will emerge. Once you have that information, we'll set a trap for them. Violet, I'm going to need you to get smaller than you've ever been. If another bug emerges, we'll be there, and you'll be the one to get close enough to extract hair and skin samples—blood, too, if you can get it. I'll be working on an analysis. Come to me as soon as you get anything."

Conrad got to his feet, setting off a flurry of move-ment and chatter. Everyone dispersed but Piper, who remained at the table, aware that she was the only team member who had nothing to do.

"Conrad?"

Conrad turned, remembering her. "Yes?"

"What should I do?"

"You'd better rest."

"But—" Piper faltered. "I'm going to be okay, aren't I? This is just temporary, and once we figure out what's wrong, I'll be able to fly again . . . right?"

Conrad paused. "Let's get more information."

WITHOUT ANYTHING TO DO, PIPER FOUND the day stretching out endlessly. Betty insisted upon feeding her, as though her trouble were due to lack of nourishment and the solution rested in a solid serving of bacon and eggs. When Piper was unable to eat a bite, Betty decided Doc Bell should take a look at her.

"It's been a long time since you've had a checkup," Betty pointed out. "It can't hurt to go see Doc Bell."

Doc Bell's office was housed in a small clapboard building off Main Street. It wasn't much more than a waiting room and an examining room, but as he was the only doctor in Lowland County, he was busy. Piper soon found herself sitting on the examining table as Doc Bell listened to her heart, checked her joints and reflexes, and then held her tongue down with a wooden tongue depressor, instructing her to say "ahhhh."

"Ahhhhh."

"Hmmmm," Doc Bell muttered, squinting at her.

Piper felt a small stirring of hope that Doc Bell was seeing something simple, maybe something that could be solved with a pill, and that as soon as she swallowed that pill she'd be able to fly home.

"Hmmmm." Finishing up, Doc Bell draped his stethoscope around his neck. "She looks normal to me," he said.

"But that's the problem; she wasn't normal before," Betty said fretfully.

"You got me there," Doc Bell agreed.

"I want to go back to the way I was," Piper said.

"Ahhhh." Doc Bell scratched the top of his head. He was getting quite old now, and his hair was white and had the habit of sticking up straight in the air when fussed with. He was a small, pensive man who had seen enough to know that life had its own agenda for doing things, and he was wise enough to get out of its way when it was doing it.

Sitting on a small rolling chair, he looked at Piper

thoughtfully. "If there's one thing I've noticed in all my years of doctoring, it's that we're all changing, either growing upward or down. It's a mighty hard thing to change a body's mind once it gets going in one direction or the other."

"But this just happened all of a sudden," Piper pointed out. "You can fix a broken leg or an arm, can't you?"

"Sure I can," Doc Bell said. "But you aren't broken. Sometimes folks just wake up one day and find their bodies aren't like they were before. It's all part of growing up."

Not for one second was Piper prepared to believe this. "Not for me and my friends it isn't."

"Well, young lady, the only thing I can tell you," said Doc Bell without rancor, "is that there's nothing wrong with you—you ain't sick; you ain't broken; you're not in any pain. I can't make you more right than a body normally is; I wasn't taught how to do that in medical school. And there's nothing wrong with being a normal, healthy girl of twelve years old. There's plenty of girls out there who'd give anything to be normal and healthy, and I happen to know a thing or two about that." Doc Bell turned to Betty. "There's something to be said for counting your blessings and just appreciating what you have. Of course, I'm old-fashioned that way, and most folks don't hold with the old ways."

"Amen to that," Betty said. Doc Bell's words made a whole lot of sense to her.

Piper felt a zing of anger. Clearly, Doc Bell was not appreciating the severity of the situation. "This," she said, pointing to her body, "is not me. I have never felt this way before. I can't live the rest of my life like this."

"Watch your mouth, Piper McCloud," Betty warned. "I won't stand for sass."

Piper had an uncontrollable urge to roll her eyes.

"There, there," Doc Bell chuckled. "These things always find a way of working themselves out in their own time, one way or the other."

———✦———

"DOC BELL'S SO OLD. HE DOESN'T UNDER-stand what I'm talking about," Piper complained when Betty pulled the ancient pickup truck to a lurching stop in front of the farmhouse.

Betty stuck out her lower lip and tightened her jaw. "Seems to me he talked good common sense. I never was much one for the flying, and maybe it'd do you some good to keep your feet on the ground."

"How exactly is that going to do me one bit of good?" Piper got out and slammed the old rusty door after her. "All I ever wanted to do was fly."

Dragging her weary body from the truck, Betty said, "God has a plan for all of us."

Piper threw up her hands. "So it was God's plan that I fly so that he could take it away from me? That doesn't make any sense." Piper turned away from her mother and stomped to the barn to find her friends. They would understand.

Inside the barn Piper found all the kids gathered in a team meeting, the air thick with concentration and plans. Conrad had a three-dimensional terrain map projected above the table. He'd already created team lists and arrows and action points. Myrtle was jotting down notes, and Jasper was nervously rubbing his hands together, making them glow without realizing he was doing it. All of which was to say it was a completely typical "save the world" team meeting.

Piper took her place opposite Conrad and tried to catch up on what she'd missed. She turned to Lily for information, but Lily was practicing telekinetically lifting up Violet, who had shrunk down to the size of a small doll.

Conrad shut down his model with a snap of his fingers. "And that wraps it up. We'll move out in fifteen minutes. Myrtle, I want boots on the ground ahead of us so that we know what we're walking into."

Myrtle saluted and zipped away. The others got to their feet, intent on assigned tasks.

"Wait!" Piper was forced to trail behind Lily, who was the last to leave, since she had to negotiate a path for Violet too. "The meeting's over already? What's going on?"

"Didn't you hear? Myrtle and Daisy figured out the coordinates on the next bug eruption. Conrad's worked out a plan for us to gather DNA from the bugs so that we can analyze it."

"Tell her about the picture!" said a mouse-like voice coming from Violet, who was floating between them.

Lily's face screwed up. "Oh yeah, and big win—Conrad uncovered this obscure cave drawing from thousands of years ago that depicts the bugs. He thinks maybe they're some sort of ancient species or something."

"Really? What did the cave drawing look like?"

Lily put Violet down on the nearest workstation and then pressed the button on a monitor. A few quick keystrokes later she pulled up a strange drawing, the sight of which stopped Piper in her tracks. With rudimentary strokes, the ancient etching depicted large bugs chasing people. A person lay on the ground, apparently dead from a bug attack. Other people were wielding spears at the bugs.

"Holy moly," Piper breathed, shaking her head. "Have you ever seen anything like this?"

"Nope," Lily answered. "I sure haven't."

Piper touched the curve on the back of the bug. It reminded her of something, but she couldn't quite think of what. For a moment she felt dizzy.

"Lily, does this bug remind you of anything?" Piper turned to Lily, but Lily was gone. All of them were gone. How long had she been standing there for?

Piper ran to the door, catching sight of the transport in the yard. The team had several different modes of getting to and from missions, and today Conrad had ordered up the trucks. They were sleek, black, unmarked, self-driving transport trucks packed full of every possible device. Generally speaking, when the kids went out on a mission, Myrtle ran, Piper flew, Nalen and Ahmed whipped up a wind and windsurfed, and everyone else traveled as a team.

"Moving out," Conrad said, closing up the back of the first truck.

Piper went for the other truck, ready to climb in. Before she could get a foothold, Conrad was at her side. "Piper, can I talk to you for one second?"

"You bet!" Piper waited expectantly for whatever it was that Conrad had to say.

Conrad hesitated, lowering his voice. "The thing is, Piper, we don't yet understand all the effects of the venom."

"I know," Piper said quickly. "But, like you said, once we get more information from the bugs, we'll be able to figure it out. Right?"

"That's my hypothesis." Conrad ran his hands through his hair and looked away. "But these missions are . . . dangerous, Piper. Without our special abilities, we could get hurt."

Piper puffed air out of her mouth. "I'm not going to get hurt."

As soon as the words escaped her mouth, it was obvious to her that this had already happened.

"Or get killed," Conrad continued. "This is not an easy mission, and the team has to be focused on the objectives, not . . ." Conrad let his words die away.

"Not on babysitting me?" A heat rose up inside Piper; her eyes narrowed. "How many missions have we done together?"

Conrad shook his head. "That's not the point."

"How many?" Piper insisted.

"What—you want a number?"

"Yes, I want an exact number! How many missions have we been on?"

Conrad threw up his hands. "Four hundred and two."

Piper crossed her arms over her chest. "And how many were successful?"

"You are not being rational right now."

"Just because you're a genius, it doesn't mean you hold the copyright on rational thinking. Our success rate?"

"Four hundred and one; I cannot count our last mission as being successful."

"Okay, so that's over ninety-nine point nine percent success."

"Ninety-nine point seven five," Conrad corrected.

"Whatever. I've been on every single one of those missions." Piper pointed to herself and back to Conrad. "It's been me and you the whole time. Together. A team."

Conrad sighed, took a step back.

Piper mounted the truck. "I don't know what's gotten into you all of a sudden."

"We need more information on this venom. I just want you to be safe," Conrad argued, but Piper was already inside.

CHAPTER

7

*T*HE TRANSPORT WAS LUXURIOUS. IT was designed to accommodate a large lounge area with workstations, a small kitchen stocked with snacks, and a few bunk beds. The other kids, who were used to riding this way, settled into their usual spots, but Piper, who always flew, had to figure out exactly where she felt comfortable. After sinking into a couch and resenting the softness, she ended up at a table where Smitty and Kimber were hard at work, bent over thick textbooks.

"Did you figure out this one?" Kimber tilted her book toward Smitty, pointing at a problem.

Smitty shook his head. "I think it has to do with the x being part of the y over the z."

"Ohhh, I see." Kimber got back to work.

Piper peeked at the books. "What's that?"

"College entrance exam." Kimber flipped her page over and started on the next one. "I'm doing a practice test. I have to do one every day to prepare. I'm applying for electrical engineering, and it's competitive to get a spot at the good schools."

"Gosh." Piper looked down at the problems Kimber was working on, and they looked hard, harder then anything she could probably ever do. "You're going to college?"

"Well, I can't make a living by shooting electrical current out of my fingertips." Kimber shrugged. "It's not exactly a paid position. I'm not saying that it's not fun saving the world, but at a certain point you have to grow up and get a job."

"She's got that right." Smitty nodded. "Having X-ray vision will only get you so far. It won't pay my rent, when I have rent, that is. That's why I'm going to apply to med school and go into radiology."

Kimber turned back to Piper. "What about you? What are you going to do?"

"Me?" Piper shifted back and forth. "Uh. I've been . . . thinking of things."

"You've got a few years yet to pick just one," Kimber said. "It's different for us. We have to get our college applications out this fall."

What was Piper going to do when she grew up? She hadn't really thought about it before. "How did you find out about electrical engineering? I mean, did someone tell you about it?" Had there been a meeting about how to live your life, and had Piper missed it?

"Smitty and I have been researching career choices for the last two years. We weighed the pros and cons between our passions, our academic strengths, and our long-term financial goals. I mean, you have to be practical, too, right?"

Piper's mouth opened, but no sound came out.

"I mean, I'm sure you've already thought about all this. It's not like we're the only ones." Kimber laughed like she was being silly. "What's on your list?"

"My list?"

"Well, what are you good at?" Kimber waited.

A day ago the first word out of Piper's mouth would have been "flying," but now she didn't know if that was true. If she didn't have flying, what did she have?

"Well, before," Piper said slowly, "I had thought about opening a flying school."

"So you want to be a teacher." Kimber clapped her hands. "Great idea! Of course, you'll have to go to teachers college and get your bachelor's of education to do that. They've got a lot of good programs, but I hear they're competitive to get into, so you'd better keep your grades up. Plus, if you specialize in something like flying, you'd probably have to get your master's, too."

"My master's?"

"Of course. You can't just go out and start a school without having the proper degrees."

"Oh." Having a flying school suddenly seemed like a difficult proposition, even if she was able to fly again. How had she not known it wasn't as simple as putting up signs and getting students? Piper looked down at the books. "I didn't know."

"What? You thought you were just going to fly around saving the planet, and that would put food on the table?" Kimber snorted.

"Hardly." Smitty laughed with her. "It's not like we're paid tips."

"Can you imagine? It was our pleasure saving you from this burning building and now give us some cash?" Kimber rolled her eyes. "Like that's going to happen. The world doesn't work that way."

"But . . ." Piper felt confused and heavy, and her lower back started to ache. "I thought we were helping out and doing good."

"Sure we are."

"Of course."

"But that's not how the grown-up world works, Piper. And sooner or later we're all going to have to grow up." Although Kimber's words were blunt and to the point, as Kimber was herself, they were not unkind. She was trying to be helpful.

It wasn't that Piper didn't appreciate her advice; it was just one more thing that she had to figure out, and her plate was already crowded with things she didn't know what to do with. The whole situation just made her feel tired.

"I think I'll get some rest," Piper said.

"Good idea! We won't get there for another couple of hours. Plenty of time to fit in several catnaps."

Kimber and Smitty returned to their studying, and Piper dragged herself up from the table and back to the too-soft couch. Gathering up a blanket, she collapsed beneath it and worried about not being able to fly, state requirements for opening up a flying school, entrance examinations for teachers college, and the fact that she'd been bitten by a bug the size of a small boulder, in no particular order.

CHAPTER

8

"THE BUGS ARE APPROXIMATELY TWENTY feet below the surface and coming up fast," Smitty reported. "There's a pod of ten—make that twelve. ETA at the surface: three minutes from now."

"Give me exact coordinates." Conrad was busy hacking into the orbiting satellite using a handheld device.

"Ten feet northwest of our current position."

Their current position was a swamp. All eleven of them were clustered together on a small mound in the middle of what felt like a witch's brew. The hot day had turned to a cold, inky night, and the water let off a thick, soupy steam. This wasn't a problem for Smitty with his X-ray vision, but the rest of them were hard-pressed to see more than a few feet in any direction.

Piper was standing closest to the water, and her feet were sopping wet. She couldn't remember the last time she'd had wet shoes or stood in a dirty swamp—that's what hovering was for. On any other mission she'd be scouting the area from above at that very moment, providing important information to the rest of the team. From where she stood now she couldn't see a darn thing.

A ripple in the swamp caught Piper's attention, and she leaned down for a closer look. It appeared that a group of fish was heading toward her. The size of the ripple in the water grew larger. Could it be a turtle? Piper bent over.

Suddenly the swamp erupted, and an alligator the size of a large log jettisoned up, its mouth wide, teeth shining. Its jaws snapped around Piper's middle. Before she even knew what was going on, even before she could scream, the alligator pulled her down into the water and away.

Back on the mound the nine other kids witnessed the attack with unflappable calm. "I'm seeing about fifteen other alligators in the area," Smitty remarked. "There's a whack of snakes around here too."

"We seriously don't have time for this," Conrad sighed. "Daisy, can you have a word with our alligator friend?"

Daisy dove into the water.

"As for the rest of you—Smitty, keep your eye on the prize. Violet, I want you down to your smallest. Lily, get into position so that you're able to maneuver Violet. Ahmed and Nalen, would you please take care of this fog and break up the cloud cover so that we can have some decent visibility?"

Once again, the water next to the mound erupted as a thrashing alligator was ejected, landing with a wet *thunk* in front of the group. Piper was still fixed in its jaws, gasping for air. Moments later, Daisy trudged out of the muddy swamp.

While Piper coughed and spluttered, Daisy stomped one thick foot onto the alligator's back, pinning it. With little effort, she next pried open its jaws, and Piper was dumped on the ground, bleeding like a stuck pig.

In short order, Jasper healed Piper, and Daisy shot-put the snappy alligator back into the swamp. Momentarily dazed, Piper remained in the wet mud, gathering herself. She got to her feet in a jerky, embarrassed way and brushed away the mud.

"It could have happened to anyone," she said weakly.

Conrad inhaled a pained, thoughtful tug of dirty swamp air through his nostrils. He wasn't about to debate Piper on that point at this time. "Move out," he said, and the kids dispatched quickly to their positions. To Piper he said, "Stay close to me. That's an order."

Sparks of fury bubbled and popped inside Piper's chest. She wasn't going to take orders from Conrad. They were a team; he wasn't her boss!

"Here they come," Smitty said over the comm. (Each

of the children had a thin silver device in their ear that linked them for easy communication.)

Sure enough, large bomb-like bubbles rocketed out of the swamp, followed quickly by the appearance of the first bug thrashing up to the surface. The sight of it instinctively made Piper's breath catch in her throat, and she took a step back.

Conrad said, "We've got a visual. Lily, that's a 'go' for Violet."

The bug was buzzing angrily in the water, pulling itself onto a stump. Once it had a foothold, it shook itself with force and stretched out its wings, roaring. There was something about the way the bug was moving that suddenly struck Piper. It was moving the way she felt inside, like it was uncomfortable to have to sit still in its own skin—like she wished she could throw her head back and roar up to the heavens her outrage and anger.

"Does it look like it's—" Piper whispered to Conrad. "Like it's in pain?"

"Shhh. I need to focus, Piper." Conrad waved Piper back and away. "Not so fast, Lily. Bring her in lower and slower. Violet, get ready to grab tissue and hair samples, but blood would be ideal. The more the better."

A second bug was now erupting from the water. This one was even closer to their position. Piper leaned in and watched carefully. The bug found footing between two rocks. It flapped its wings.

Piper moved her arms, imitating the flap.

Using its two front legs, the bug clawed at its chest in thrashing, angry movements.

Piper did the same, and it felt good to her. It felt like relief.

The bug spread its wings, and with a wicked thrust, it pulled its bulky weight up, up, up.

Piper raised her arms, willing herself up, up, up. She could not follow, but she felt compelled upward. Her whole body felt the burning need to ascend.

As the second bug lifted off, another bug emerged behind them, closer still. When the water settled around it, Piper could see that this bug was smaller, much smaller, than the others. This bug was hardly bigger than a beach ball, and it latched on to a floating log with difficulty. Then came the roar and the flapping of its wings.

As it prepared to ascend, Piper saw a telltale ripple in the water coming right at the log the little bug floated on.

"Go, go," she urged the bug. "Fly away."

The bug flapped its wings, but it wasn't strong, not like the last one. It lifted off the log and maintained a low altitude for a short burst before falling back down.

The ripple was moving quickly.

"Hurry! Hurry!"

The baby bug flapped its wings as hard as it might. The ripple was on it.

Piper yelled, "Fly away!"

The bug reached up.

The alligator erupted from the water, its mouth wide.

A thin, high squeal came out of the bug when the jaws of the alligator snapped shut. The sound pierced Piper's eardrums like a knife.

The bug fought against the alligator, and the alligator fought back. Suddenly the red belly of the bug ignited.

Piper fell to her knees.

At once Conrad was beside her, and she could see his mouth moving but wasn't able to hear what he was saying. All she could hear was a whispering chirp. She could not understand its meaning, but it felt like it was not only outside her but inside her, and it felled her with a sharp, stabbing pain.

The alligator was dragging the bug down. The bug had freed a wing and was flapping it. The belly of the bug was fire-engine red, about to blow.

Conrad reached out to Piper, touching her stomach. Piper looked down and saw that she was glowing red too. Out of her belly and back came the same glow as the bug's.

Conrad's lips moved urgently now.

Piper turned away from him and back to the bug as the alligator dragged it down one last time. It did not come back to the surface. The red light flickered and then went dim.

Piper fell to the ground.

———◆———

LATER, ON THE SOFT COUCH OF THE TRANS-port, Piper regained consciousness. Everyone was gathered around her, eyes serious and watching.

Piper felt her stomach. "What happened?"

"That's what we want to know." Conrad's arms were crossed over his chest.

"It's like you were on fire," Jasper said softly. "Like you were burning up from the inside."

Piper wrapped her arms around the place where embers of heat still smoldered. "I—I didn't do anything. It just happened to me. I couldn't control it."

Ahmed let out a low whistle, and Nalen shook his head. Worried glances were exchanged right and left.

"It looked like there was a connection between you and the bug," Conrad pointed out. "Like it was communicating with you. You were glowing at the same time and in the same rhythm."

Piper thought about the strange chirping sound she

had heard in her head and the other feelings that she had begun to feel since she'd been bitten.

"There is scientific evidence that some animals and insects communicate using sonic frequencies we can't access," Conrad continued. "They have a hive mentality and act as a collective."

"What does that mean?"

"It means that the bugs are communicating with you, and during the alligator attack you reacted in the same way they did. You lost control."

"That can't be true." Piper shook her head and looked to Kimber, who could usually be counted on to back her up. The look on Kimber's face told Piper she wasn't going to get the support she was looking for. "I am not being controlled by the bugs!" Piper said.

"I'm not saying they are controlling you," Conrad corrected. "I'm pointing out the fact that they are communicating with you and that you are responding to the communications that they are sending."

"But I'm fine. I am." Piper got to her feet. "It won't happen again. It was just a fluke."

Her remark was met with silence.

"Really," Piper insisted. "I'm fine."

CHAPTER

9

JOE McCLOUD USED THE FORCE OF HIS weight to push his shovel into the soil, scooping out a helping and then going back for more. He did this over and over again. Joe was a sycamore tree of a man: lean and silent, weathered and strong. He liked the steadiness of farmwork and the feeling he had at the end of the day when he returned his weary body to the kitchen and Betty placed a hearty plate of good food in front of him. His life was uncomplicated and honest, like his nature. But more than anything, Joe McCloud loved his child.

It pained him to see Piper now, perched like a baby bird on a nearby rock, watching him work. After the events of the last week, she was a shadow of her normally buoyant self.

"Pa, can I tell you something?"

Joe shoveled to a steady rhythm, waiting on Piper's words.

"Nothing's working." Piper's chest heaved up and down several times before she could manage to get a handle on herself again.

"I've tried everything. I truly have. I jumped off anything I could find; then I stayed real still and thought about the sky. I tried to run into flying too." She shook her head sadly, thinking about how that didn't work, either. "Everyone's doing everything they can to help me. Daisy used all her strength to throw me way up in the air. Lily telekinetically dangled me under the clouds to see if that would start it up again. Conrad made some wings, then got Ahmed and Nalen to start a windstorm, and they flew me like a kite. Smitty cooked up a catapult and shot me into the air. Kimber even tried shock therapy. That hurt.

"But none of it worked." Piper let out a jagged sigh. "I've got to face the fact that I might never fly again."

Joe looked up sharply, and Piper put up her hand. "I know what you're gonna say: if I give it time, it might come back. Conrad says the same thing. You know I'm not someone who gives up, and I'm not giving up now, either." Piper's hand felt the place in her stomach that had a knowing. "But I don't feel like I used to. It feels like the sky isn't in me anymore."

Joe shoveled thoughtfully, sadly. Piper wound her arms around herself, hugging her midsection.

"And the worst part of it is that I think it's my fault."

Joe stopped working.

Piper's face was all storm clouds. "I'm not saying that I wanted that bug to bite me or that I don't want to fly. No, it's not that at all. But things are different now. Everything is changing. And I'm getting to be different too, so that sometimes I hardly know who I am. Take last Sunday, when the preacher announced the spring dance. Before, I would have been real excited about getting ice cream or making friends, but when I heard about it, all I could think of was that I didn't have a nice dress to wear and that I wanted to look pretty. And then I got to worrying about the fact that maybe no one would invite me to the dance. You see, Jasper asked Lily to go with him, then Smitty asked Kimber, but no one asked me. I thought Con—Well, I thought maybe someone would ask me to go. But he didn't."

Piper tugged at her hair like she was angry at it, like it was the problem. "I'm twelve years old. I'm going to be thirteen in a few months, and my hair's always flying around like it's got a mind of its own. I'm not a child anymore."

Piper chewed on her lip, considering all the things

one has to consider when they are on the verge of being grown-up.

"Lily said that I need to wear my hair down more. She said that I should put on a dress, and then maybe Con—maybe someone would invite me to the dance. But the trouble is, if you're flying and you leave your hair down, it gets in your face so that you can't see. Plus, it's so windy my dress flies up, and I've got to hold it down. Then when Max got up to no good and I was flying around, I couldn't see the way I normally do, so I didn't spot Jasper until it was too late. Then I was slow flying to get to him because I had to hold my dress down."

Piper sighed out her regret and frustration and disappointment.

"Sure, I saved Jasper, but it was my fault he got into trouble in the first place. If I'd braided my hair back like I normally do and had a good pair of jeans on, we wouldn't have been where we shouldn't, and I wouldn't have gotten bit. And that's the truth.

"I want to fly fast and be strong, but I want to be invited to the dance, too. And now I can't fly and I'm not going to the dance and I've ruined everything."

Joe put his shovel down and went to Piper.

"I just don't know what I'm gonna do if I never get

to fly again." Piper's voice was thin and hollow. "It makes my whole body ache to think about it. What am I going to do, Pa?"

Joe McCloud put his arms around his broken bird and held her close. Piper sighed and leaned into him.

CHAPTER

10

At some point in the middle of the night, as often happened, there was an emergency. For all the years the kids had been together, it always went down the same way: a specially designed monitoring system was triggered by a disaster or calamity; the warning system woke Conrad; Conrad woke the others.

That night, nobody woke Piper. When she came down to breakfast, she found Fido scrounging around the empty kitchen and instantly knew they'd left her behind. Not one of them had thought to wake her. Or worse, they had thought about it and decided not to.

Piper plunked herself down at the kitchen table and sulked. A slumped-over human was a perfect target for a ravenous pet, and Fido flapped his leathery wings until he was on the table in front of Piper's face. When she didn't pat him, he gave her a few prickly licks from his purple tongue.

"They left us, Fido."

Fido snurfled around Piper, trying to figure out where she was hiding food.

"They didn't even wake me up! Couldn't they have at least said good-bye and told me when they'd be back?"

Fido offered another lick, slurping her across the chin.

Piper pet him consolingly. "You're left behind a lot, huh? I guess I am too, now."

A line of drool came out of the side of Fido's mouth. For the love of all that was holy, would she not feed him a morsel of something?

"Do you want a Fido Treat?"

Fido did indeed want a Fido Treat. More than he could possibly communicate with his grumbling bark and his smushed-up, wrinkly face. He flew about the kitchen excitedly, knocking into things until Piper gave him two treats in his bowl, and he crouched down and gobbled and crunched.

As it happened, it was a Sunday. For Betty, the Lord's day was all about church, and come rain or shine she saw to it that the McClouds were present and accounted for lest there was someone taking attendance in a loftier sphere. As though the day had no end to its anomalies, Betty McCloud didn't feel up to going to church. Joe didn't want to leave her side, and so Piper was sent off as the sole representative of the McCloud clan.

Walking down Creek Road, the first farm Piper passed, and the McCloud's nearest neighbors, was the Miller farm. The Millers were also on their way to church, but when they saw Piper, they pushed on ahead and didn't greet her or acknowledge her in any way. This was far from an anomaly.

After the Miller farm was a long stretch of neatly planted corn and wheat fields that led into a thicket of trees. Past the thicket was Main Street, at the head of which stood the church. Lowland County Church was a white clapboard building, ample enough to hold the small congregation of farmers and their children, its one claim to grandness being a tall steeple, a sure signal to the Almighty that Lowland County worshippers meant business.

Today was the first time that Piper had walked the entire distance to town without floating or flying. By the time she reached the thicket of trees, her feet ached and her leg muscles complained. Walking, Piper decided as she leaned up against a tree to rest, was her least favorite thing to do. Another reason to add to her very long list of why flying was better.

As she rested, Piper caught sight of an old woman hobbling down a forest path carrying an electric blender.

In the same way that everyone in Lowland County knew all there was to know about Piper and her flying, Piper knew all about this old woman.

She had been born and christened with the name Bertie Becca, but the name hadn't stuck. She'd been an odd baby who grew into an odder child, so that by the time she was an adult, she'd turned full-blown strange. She wasn't strange in the way Piper was strange, though; she had a different variety of it that was all her own.

Bertie once said that the wind had told her to cut her hair, and she'd shorn her head like a sheep and then covered it in goose fat to hold her body heat in. She was a rather shocking and smelly sight around Lowland County after that. Another time, she had an argument with a strawberry bush and returned to yell at it every afternoon for a week until it died.

When she was a teenager, Bertie had a dream that a snake was eating her heart out. At the last moment a raven swooped down and pecked the snake away. This, she claimed, was a sure sign that her true name was Raven, and she demanded that she be called such. The Lowland County boys were delighted and took to calling her Stark Raven Mad. The name stuck, in a shorter version, and one and all, including the minister, called her Stark Raven until people could hardly remember that Bertie Becca had ever been her given name.

The problem with Stark Raven was not her eccentricities or her strangeness but her brilliance. For about one in ten things she did had the stroke of absolute genius. Like the time she had stopped a swarm of locusts from eating all the Lowland County crops by offering them a cup of sweet tea. The locusts drank the tea and flew away, never to return.

True story.

Then there was the time that eight-year-old Dukie Dick went missing, and no one could find him. Out of desperation, his parents begged Stark Raven for help, and she'd gotten down on her hands and knees in the middle of Main Street and put her ear to the ground. When she got back on her feet, she told Dukie Dick's parents that he'd fallen down the well behind old man Decater's house. Sure enough, that's just where they found him. Later everyone asked Stark Raven how she knew this. "Simple," she said. "There was a worm in the ground next to my ear, and he told me."

Folks in Lowland County didn't have a large tolerance, or any tolerance really, for the eccentricities of a person like Stark Raven, but they kept her around as a sort of insurance on the off chance things got really bad and she could save them from calamity.

But while Stark Raven wasn't driven off, she wasn't particularly welcomed, either. No one talked to her, children were not allowed anywhere near her, and she was expected to keep to herself. As it happened, this suited Stark Raven just fine. She settled in a shack covered by vines and herbs in the thicket of trees and let her hair grow wild and matted down her back. The only time folks in Lowland County thought about Stark Raven was when they got themselves in a pickle of such a nature that there was no help for it, and then, like blazes, they beat a path to her door, begging for a miracle and praying it would work and not be some batty, weird crap. She was known for that, too.

PIPER COULD HEAR THE CHURCH BELLS ringing and knew she had best get a move on, but the sight of Stark Raven pulled her like a magnet.

She could hear Betty's words in her head. "Don't you go near that Stark Raven, Piper! Leave her be."

Yet still . . .

Before Piper knew what she was doing, her tired feet and aching legs were walking with a sure step down the path that led to Stark Raven's shack.

CHAPTER

11

$\mathcal{A}$ ROUND THE CURVE OF THE TRAIL, THE trees in the ticket grew dense so that it was dim and cast in a mossy glow. Until that morning, Piper had obeyed Betty's decree to keep away from Stark Raven, making this the only place in Lowland County she had never been. Even from the sky it wasn't possible to see through the trees, so Piper had no idea what she was walking into.

The trail was well worn, curving and ambling on tangents, hugged closely on either side by the forest. When it felt as though she had passed out of Lowland County entirely, Piper came to two large stones on either side of the path that formed a gateway. On the other side of this natural gate, Piper found herself in a glade. It was not much larger than the McCloud barn, covered by the boughs of the nearby ancient trees, giving it the feeling of an outdoor cathedral. The first things that caught Piper's eye were wind chimes made of sticks and stones that hung from the trees. When the wind passed through them, they clicked and clacked like happy typewriters.

In the center of the clearing was a tumbledown shack, surrounded on all sides by a hodgepodge collection of the strangest, most unexpected things that only Stark Raven herself understood and saw the need for.

To Piper's right stood a brand-new silver range. It looked expensive. It gleamed like a chalice and stood as though waiting for a top chef to appear and start whipping up a soufflé. A raccoon family had taken up residence in the oven part of the range, and there was a raccoon-size letterbox, to which someone, Piper guessed Stark Raven, had delivered letters. The letters were also raccoon size.

To her left, bunches of herbs and flowers were threaded up on large drying racks and then, inexplicably right in front of the shack, which was no bigger than a large room, was a hot-pink chaise longue. It was upon this that Stark Raven was currently reclining, talking in a heated fashion to a mouse that was perched upon her knee.

"No," she told the mouse firmly, holding up her gnarled finger. "The internet is connected to the plumbing, and the electricity requires postage. I've told you this before."

The mouse flicked his tale angrily and sat up on his hind legs.

"If you want rain, then don't eat nuts," Stark Raven told him.

"Ummmm-hum," Piper said, politely clearing her throat.

The mouse and Stark Raven looked to her, and neither of them was in the least bit surprised to find her there.

"I was passing by," Piper explained, because it seemed like an explanation might be in order. "I was going to church. I thought I should stop and say hello." She waved her fingers about. "Hello."

Stark Raven fixed her with a firm look. "You haven't ever stopped in to say hello before."

Piper felt all at once that she had been inexcusably mean and thoughtless. Perhaps Stark Raven wanted to have visitors and was lonely. Why had she never thought of that? "I'm sorry."

Stark Raven squinted, taking a good look at Piper. "You're that Piper McCloud."

"Yes."

"You've sprung up and got tall. You're almost full-grown. That Millie Mae Miller says you'll be the death of us all. She says you got the devil in you."

"I—I don't have the devil in me," Piper stammered. It chapped Piper to no end the way Millie Mae went about saying things like that. "Millie Mae Miller shouldn't say things that aren't true."

Stark Raven laughed at this in a hooting sort of way. "Folks can't speak truth if they don't got the truth in 'em." With effort, she hoisted herself up and off the recliner, chuckling as she did so.

Piper felt discombobulated and unhinged. Was it impolite to have invited herself into the glade? What was she supposed to do now?

"I can fly," Piper blurted out.

"I know that," Stark Raven said.

"But I had an accident, and now I can't fly anymore. I don't know what to do."

"Ahhh." Stark Raven nodded her head as though this was all making sense. "So you came to ask for my help."

And Piper was startled to realize that this was exactly why she had come. "Oh. Yes. Do you think . . . I was wondering . . . I mean, can you help me?"

Stark Raven took a hard look at Piper and didn't

blink. It felt to Piper like her eyes were probing unseen places.

"Hmm," she said, snapping back to the glade. "Best come inside."

Stark Raven hobbled to her shack, but Piper hesitated to follow her.

"Come or don't. Don't bother me none," Stark Raven said. "But if you want my help, this is where you'll find it."

Piper looked over her shoulder, took a fortifying breath, and cautiously followed Stark Raven.

The inside of the shack was not unlike the outside but for the fact that it was surprisingly neat and uncluttered. A small cot of a bed was wedged in one corner. A large wood table dominated the center of the room, and a cooking area of sorts was to the right of the entrance and framed by two windows.

"Sit yourself down," Stark Raven said without turning. She selected two clay cups and a tiny delicate china bowl decorated with a single red flower out of her cupboard. She placed these items on the table and then went to a large pantry stocked with herbs and jars. Piper could spy chicken feet floating about in a green liquid and pigs eyes in another and things too hideous to even contemplate in more.

Piper perched on the edge of the chair closest to the door.

"You gonna tell me what happened?" Stark Raven didn't pause in her efforts. "I can't read minds."

"Oh, I'm sorry. There was a bug, a big bug, and it bit me." Piper twisted and pointed to her back. "Right here. Ever since then I haven't been able to fly."

"Uh-huh. I can see," she said, without looking up at Piper, "that your insides are all scrambled up, like an egg."

This was news to Piper. "I'm scrambled?"

"Uh-huh." The old woman shook her head. "It's like you aren't yourself anymore."

"Yes," Piper said excitedly. "That's just it."

"The flying is still inside you, but you got to figure out where you put it."

"How do I do that?"

"Don't ask me." Stark Raven shrugged. "Only you can know where it is."

"But I don't! I don't know! I've tried and tried to fly, and I can't. I've done everything."

"Ha. Getting yourself up into the air won't help. Flying happens last. It's the result of what comes before." Stark Raven stood looking at Piper and not doing much else. Piper was anxious to come to a solution and considered the things in front of her.

"Maybe you can give me something to drink, or a special stone that'll make my flying come back?"

Stark Raven snorted indelicately. "Wouldn't that be nice and easy!"

"Or maybe you know a spell or have words that I can say?"

Stark Raven eyed Piper angrily. "What d'ya take me for, a witch?"

Piper bit her lip and looked down.

Stark Raven picked up the large stone that sat on the edge of the table and smashed it on the delicate china bowl. The bowl instantly shattered into tiny bits.

Startled, Piper yelped, half rising.

Stark Raven reached for the pieces of the bowl and gathered them up. "This bowl is your flying," she said. "This rock here is the bite you got." Now that she had all the pieces of the bowl in her hand, she walked to the open window and threw them outside into the forest. "That's where your flying is. It's everywhere. But inside you. It's up to you to gather all the pieces of it back together and put them right. Soon as you do that, you'll fly again."

Piper's ballooning hope burst inside her, and she slumped over. "But how am I going to do that?"

"Beats me," Stark Raven cackled, and shook her head at the impossibility of it all. "Don't see how you can."

Piper burst into tears. Not only was she upset, but she was embarrassed to be crying like a baby, and she spread her hands over her face to hide herself.

Stark Raven sighed. "There, there, child. Crying isn't going to help you."

"But I just *have* to fly. It's all I ever wanted. I miss being up in the sky, and if I don't fly, my friends won't want nothing to do with me, and I'm so lonesome for the sky I could just split down the middle." Piper's sobs came with hiccups. "Please, can't you do something?"

Piper presented such a pitiful picture that Stark Raven shook her head again, and then took a small bottle from a cupboard and put it on the table in front of Piper.

"I wasn't going to offer this up, but seeing as you have your heart set on it . . ." She slid the bottle before Piper, who was so upset she hardly noticed. "If you can't calm yourself some, then you won't hear what I have to say. I means to help you as best I can, but if you don't stop your howling, no one will be able to help you with anything."

With the greatest effort, Piper took one deep breath followed by another. "I'm sorry," she sobbed. "I'm not worth nothing without my flying."

"Now, that ain't true. Flying is something you do, not what you are. You hear?"

Piper nodded, hiccupping.

"Now, here. This isn't a magic potion"—Stark Raven nodded at the bottle—"but it'll unscramble you some and clean out your insides. You can't be light when you're so weighted down. This should lighten you up."

Piper wrapped her hands around the bottle gratefully. Opening the top, she peeped in and discovered an eyedropper in the cap. "Th-thank you, Miss Raven," Piper hiccupped. "Thank you so much."

"It's powerful stuff," Stark Raven warned. "Put two drops on your tongue at sunrise and sunset. No more, no less."

Piper held the bottle to her chest.

Church bells rang in the distance, and suddenly Piper's true purpose of the day returned to her. "I have to—"

"I know, I know." Stark Raven waved her hand. "You was on your way to church. Go! Go."

"Thank you. Thank you so much." Piper meant it from the bottom of her heart.

Stark Raven waved Piper away, coming to the door to watch her go. "I'll talk to my friends and see if I can't find out more about these bugs for you," she called. "No promises, but I'll do what I can."

"Thank you," Piper said again, and passed through the two rocks and found her way onto the path. When she came to the road, Piper stopped to look in the bottle. Whatever was inside was such a curious shade of blue, like the sky after a storm. Stark Raven had told her to place two drops on her tongue. Using the dropper, Piper did just that. One drop. Two drops.

At first it tasted sweet, but a few swallows later a bitter aftertaste puckered her mouth.

Starting for church, Piper suddenly realized her tongue was feeling tingly. It was a feeling she knew well—the same feeling she used to get all over her body right before she flew. The tingling didn't last long, but it filled Piper with longing.

When she came to the end of the thicket and Main Street was in front of her, Piper took out the bottle for a second time. Maybe just two more drops would be the ticket. Stark Raven said it unscrambled her. Would she be able to start flying when that happened? Maybe it would turn out to be as simple as that.

Piper took another drop. Then another.

More tingling.

On Main Street, Piper paused outside Jameson's Dry Goods and Feed long enough for a few more drops.

The tingling was moving from her throat down her

neck. Soon it would be in her stomach. If she wasn't mistaken, she was actually feeling buoyant.

Piper skipped the rest of the way to church, thinking that maybe, just maybe, on the way home she might be able to manage a little bit of floating.

CHAPTER

12

MINISTER BROWN HAD ALREADY launched into his sermon, so Piper quietly found her way into the McCloud pew and settled herself. The Millers had the pew right in front of theirs, and Millie Mae made a point of eyeing Piper so that the she wouldn't think her tardiness had gone unnoticed. Piper was careful to sit neatly and quietly and keep her eyes directly in front of her at all times so Millie Mae would not have additional fodder to add to her report.

Despite Piper's reverent appearance, her mind was imagining the faces of the other kids when they saw her fly again. Boy, would they be surprised. And they'd probably be sorry, too, that they'd left her behind today. Perhaps they'd be riddled with guilt, even. Of course, Piper would forgive them right off, but it was still satisfying to consider how bad they'd feel and maybe they'd even cry some over it.

Piper was well into imagining a scenario where Lily was weeping and begging to renew their friendship while at the same time Conrad was calling himself a louse and a heel for leaving her behind. And she, Piper, was standing like a saint, in a snow-white dress with a beam of sunshine blessing the top of her head, refusing to be angry or cast blame. No, she was all forgiveness.

It was right at this part of her fantasy that Piper realized she was feeling quite hot all of a sudden. She unfastened the top button on her dress to get some more air, and when that wasn't relief enough, she did the same to the button beneath it. Clearly, she'd run too fast to church, and the day was hotter than she'd considered.

A minute later Piper was sure the church must be on fire. Yet no one else was suffering; not a single person had so much as a bead of sweat on their brow.

The heat kept getting turned up, and now Piper felt as though she were sitting on a raging bonfire. She rolled up the sleeves on her dress and pushed down her knee socks. It still wasn't enough. With nothing else to loosen, she snatched up the hymnal in front of her and used it to fan herself.

Millie Mae did not approve of hymnals being used as

fanning mechanisms. It was disrespectful and distracting. She pursed her lips and cleared her throat loudly so that her opinion on the matter would be known.

Oblivious to Millie Mae's objections, Piper fanned faster, taking deep breaths in through her nose and out through her mouth.

Millie Mae inwardly seethed, biting her tongue while she clenched and unclenched her hand. Piper McCloud was causing a racket! If she were Millie Mae's child, she'd see to it, right quick, that she stopped this nonsense once and for all. What was that? Piper was panting like a dog now? This was Millie Mae's breaking point.

Swiveling around in her seat, Millie Mae opened her mouth to tell Piper McCloud exactly what was on her mind, but when she caught sight of Piper's face, she froze. What she saw drove all words out of her mouth and thoughts out of her head.

Piper McCloud's face had erupted in huge, bubbling boils, each one the size of a meatball. The boils were also poking out of her arms and legs and down her neck. The child was erupting like a volcano.

"Lord save us!" Millie Mae shrieked, getting to her feet.

It was at that precise moment that the largest of

Piper's boils, which was on her forehead, popped under the extreme pressure of its aggressive growth and spewed pus all over Millie Mae.

"AGGGGH!" Millie Mae screamed. "That child is possessed by the devil. LOOK—AT—HER!"

The look on Millie Mae Miller's face, combined with the explosion on her forehead, tipped Piper off to the fact that there was something more going on than a simple case of being overheated.

Piper ran from the church and didn't stop running until she got home—even though there were several boils that exploded on the way.

Betty, who'd started to feel better, was in the kitchen working on Sunday dinner when she saw Piper running up the front field toward the house.

"What in the name of—"

Piper came flying into the kitchen, her hands covering her face. "Ma! Ma, I think I'm gonna explode."

"What's happened?"

Piper threw herself on the floor. "I went to Stark Raven and she gave me something. I thought it might help me fly but now my body's gone crazy and everyone saw me and I don't know what to do."

Betty sat down with a thud, putting her hand over her forehead. "Piper McCloud! I leave you alone for one hour, and this is what you get up to?"

Piper started to cry in earnest. "But I thought if I took it . . . I thought I'd . . ."

"Let me see what you took! Show it to me!" Betty held out her hand.

Piper slid the bottle out of her pocket and relinquished it to Betty. Betty unscrewed the top, took a whiff, and jerked her head back.

"What in the blazes is this?"

Piper shook her head, her eyes wide. "I don't know. I didn't ask. Stark Raven said it would unscramble me."

Betty turned the bottle upside down. It was completely empty. "How much did you take?"

"A bit. Once I got started . . . I wanted to fly . . . I thought . . . I thought—"

"Piper McCloud, I swear you don't have a patch of common sense in your head. Oh, child. Stop your crying. You know most of the stuff Stark Raven does is plum bonkers. Thank the Lord she's no murderer, though. Whatever she gave you won't kill you, but you'll just have to wait until it runs its course."

Betty drew a warm bath for Piper and filled it with Epsom salt, which stung but also soothed her raging skin. Afterward, Betty wrapped Piper in a cool, clean sheet and gave her plenty of liquids. As she suspected, by bedtime Piper was "popped" out, but in place of the boils were angry red pimples covering every inch of her body. The look and feel of them horrified Piper.

"Now I'm worse than I was before," she wailed. "What am I gonna do, Ma?"

"You'll stop this nonsense and let yourself be," Betty sniffed. "Listen to me, child. Whether you like it or not, you can't fly right now. There's no telling if that's going to change anytime soon, and so it's up to you to find a way to make yourself useful without your flying. You hear me?"

"But, Ma . . ."

"No 'buts.' Idle hands do the devil's work. Stop mooning around and find something to do to keep yourself busy. I hope to goodness you've learned your lesson this time. You hear?"

"Yes, ma'am."

CHAPTER

13

WHILE PIPER WAS FAST ASLEEP that night, the team returned from their mission. They'd had a late night, but Conrad was still up before dawn and already hard at work when Piper found him in the barn.

"You're back!"

Conrad kept his attention focused. "Hi, Piper. Things are moving fast, and we have a lot on the go. Sorry we didn't get a chance to let you know we were leaving. It seemed better to let you rest."

Piper came up behind Conrad and peeked over his shoulder. "What's going on?"

Conrad had created three-dimensional computer images that were projected up into the air around him. He was manipulating a strand of DNA and isolating certain areas, then pausing to pull out data from them.

"The bugs are crawling out of the ground from everywhere around the planet now. Whatever it is Max started has set off a chain reaction. They're coming faster and faster." Conrad spoke absently, his mind on his task. "I'm tracking them and seeing if there is a pattern. It could be important."

Piper leaned in, getting in Conrad's way. "Look at this!" She reached out and stuck her finger in a brightly colored DNA strand.

"No, Piper, don't touch—"

Piper poked it anyway. It flickered and then disappeared altogether. Behind them, electrical sparks firecrackered out of the mainframe.

Conrad jumped to his feet, throwing up his hands. "You can't touch it, Piper. It can only handle one operator at a time or the system overloads. You know that!"

Clutching her offending finger, Piper winced. "Sorry. I forgot. I just wanted to help."

Piper waited for Conrad's fury, but he just looked at her sadly, like she was a guest he had to use his best manners with, or a small child who had to be treated with gentleness. "Don't worry about it," he said. "I'll reboot the mainframe, reload the operating system, and start again. It'll only take me a few hours."

Now Piper felt lower than a snake's belly. "I can help. Let me help."

"No!" Conrad said quickly. "No, I—I need you to . . . We really need someone to . . ."

"Yes?"

What exactly could Conrad have Piper do? "I've been noticing that everyone is getting very dehydrated," he said at last. "Can you fetch a jug of water and some glasses?"

"Fetch water?" Piper bit her lower lip. "Sure, Conrad, I can get water."

"And, Piper?"

"Yes?"

"Smitty tells me there's a dance coming up."

Piper's breath caught in her throat. "A dance?"

"Yes, a dance. Some local thing in a barn. That's good timing for us; I want to run drills over Main Street when no one is around. Can you let the others know?"

Piper swallowed hard and nodded.

Turning his back, Conrad got busy with his work, and Piper slunk out of the barn and into the yard. As she approached the house, she spotted Myrtle talking to Daisy on the porch outside the kitchen. The sight of them made her spirits rise—good old Myrtle and Daisy.

Since the time the two girls had first met, they'd been fast friends, and while Myrtle was normally shy, around Daisy she turned into a chatterbox. This morning in particular she had a lot to say.

"Conrad asked me to run all the way to New York," Myrtle told Daisy excitedly, the enthusiasm in her voice carrying across the yard to Piper. "He said there were multiple bug sightings in Central Park, and he needed me to gather samples."

"At night?"

"Yes, last night. It's not really safe for me to run in the dark, but since Piper can't fly, it had to be me. I made it in record time and got more information than Conrad even asked for and—"

Piper stepped on a twig. It snapped loudly.

Spotting Piper, Myrtle abruptly stopped talking and pushed her hair down over her eyes. Daisy blushed.

"Hi, Piper," Daisy said awkwardly with a half wave, which was equally strange.

"Hi." Piper felt oddly uncomfortable. Why did she suddenly feel like an outsider in her own home?

"It's a nice morning," Myrtle mumbled.

Piper looked up at the drab, gray sky. "Uh-huh."

A thick silence lingered between them.

"You look good today, Piper." Daisy tugged at her ear nervously. "You look . . . healthy."

"Yes," agreed Myrtle quickly. "Healthy and . . . well rested."

Piper looked down at herself. Despite the fact that

she was covered in angry red pimples, she looked the same way she always did. "Thanks."

Piper waited for Myrtle to finish her story, but when she didn't, she decided to help things along. "Did something happen last night?"

"No." Myrtle waved it away. "It was nothing."

"Huh. Well, you sounded pretty excited." Piper felt confused. "It sounded like something important."

"It wasn't. Same old, same old. You know."

Piper didn't know. She waited for them to tell her, but Daisy and Myrtle didn't.

"Well, we have to get going." Daisy gestured vaguely at some point in the field as though there was something they urgently had to attend to there.

"Yes," Myrtle agreed. "We don't want to be late."

The two girls took off, disappearing from view.

Piper found herself alone in the yard. Where was everyone?

Scratching her head, Piper walked to the house, thinking about how a week ago the story Myrtle had been telling Daisy was one she would have shared with Piper, too. Of course, a week ago, when she could fly, Conrad would have sent her to New York to collect data, and she would have been the one to return bursting with news and information.

Swinging open the screen door, Piper stopped in her tracks—the kitchen was empty.

"Ma?" Piper held the door in confusion.

Mornings used to always be Betty McCloud's "go time" of the day; up before dawn, she was a whirlwind of cooking and baking and cleaning and getting the farm awake. This morning, the kitchen was as quiet as a tomb.

"Ma?"

"I'm in here," came Betty's muffled voice from the parlor.

Piper followed the sound and found her mother lying on the couch, a cold compress covering her eyes and forehead. "Ma? Are you sick?"

"No, no. Just not feeling like myself," Betty said weakly. "Thought I'd rest up a bit till I don't feel so dizzy."

Over the last month or so Betty had taken to resting throughout the day, and when she wasn't resting, she moved more slowly, like she was wading through mud. This was the first Piper was hearing about dizziness, though. "Maybe I should run and get Doc Bell . . ."

"No, no. It ain't serious. It's nothing. I best get break-fast going." Betty took the cloth off her head and started to sit up. She got no more than halfway before a groan took her, and she returned to a reclining position.

"You don't look so good," Piper said, worried.

"Would you look at the time! Mr. McCloud will be in for his coffee soon, and I don't have a blessed thing ready."

"Well, I can do it! I can help! Let me do it."

"No, no." Once again, Betty tried to sit up and, once again, had to lie back down. "You haven't so much as boiled an egg, Piper McCloud. You've spent all your time flying here and there and haven't given one thought to kitchen work."

"Oh, but I've watched you lots of times," Piper insisted. "I can do it. You'll see."

Before Betty could stop her, Piper rushed back to the kitchen and got to work, determined to cook up a breakfast that no one would soon forget!

Piper decided on pancakes and bran muffins with bacon and eggs. This was pretty standard fare in the mornings on the McCloud farm; she'd seen Betty whip it together a million times. Easy peasy.

Piper grabbed a salad bowl and tossed in an egg and started to beat it. Those rascally eggshells got into the mix, but Piper shrugged it off: they'd add to the flavor. Betty only ever used one egg, but Piper thought two would be better and then added a third, because you can't get too much of a good thing. With each egg came more eggshells. When the batter was ready, there was no denying that it had a very lumpy quality. There was no time to dwell on that, though, because Piper had to make up the muffins too.

When Joe had finished milking the cows, he walked into the kitchen to find Piper covered in flour and the place littered with coffee grinds, eggshells, smears of butter, and puddles of milk. On the stove, the bacon was sizzling like a forest fire, and Piper was wrangling pancakes that seemed to have developed minds of their own.

Piper quickly poured Joe a cup of coffee. "Here you go, Pa. Drink it while it's hot!"

Joe gratefully took the cup but stopped short when he caught sight of the gritty, mud-like liquid in the cup. His brow twisted into a concerned knot.

"Oh, wait—you take it with sugar," Piper said, misinterpreting his expression. She grabbed the sugar bowl and tipped it to the side, depositing a generous mound on the top. The coffee was so thick, it easily supported the sugar.

"There you go." Piper ushered Joe to his seat. "Now, you sit down, and I'll get your breakfast up lickety-split."

The bacon started to catch fire, and so Piper quickly jostled the pan just as Kimber and Smitty came bursting into the kitchen with Jasper and Lily on their heels.

Lily was immediately alarmed and took a defensive posture when she caught sight of the state of the kitchen. "Are we under attack? Is it Max?"

"Geez, you'd think you'd never seen someone cook before," said Piper, laughing it off. "Sit down. Sit down. Breakfast is ready."

Nalen and Ahmed came pushing into the kitchen next and, like the others, stopped in their tracks. "This could be named a national disaster site."

"Or a hazardous waste dump."

Piper put her hands on her hips. "Do you want breakfast or not?"

The twins sat down.

Conrad was the last to find his chair, and by that time everyone was sitting with plates of food in front of them. Each plate contained two blackened strips that at one point had been bacon but were now Group 1 carcinogens; a hard, rubbery ball that Piper kept calling a pancake; and eggs so runny they appeared to be yellow soup.

"Eat up," Piper urged. "Don't be shy. Growing bodies have to eat!"

Conrad resolutely picked up his fork. He nudged Smitty, who was sitting next to him, and Smitty very reluctantly picked up his fork too.

"Thanks, Piper. This is quite a . . . breakfast." Conrad's smile made his face look pained. He sharply nudged Smitty one more time.

"Mmmmm," Smitty agreed.

Most mornings, the kids ate like wild animals, shoving food in their mouths and grabbing for seconds and thirds so that Betty had a hard time keeping up with their appetites. That morning, the kids poked and pushed at the contents of their plates in miserable silence.

"It's not going to eat itself." Piper's smile began to falter. "Try the bacon, Daisy. I made it crispy, the way you like it."

Unable to avoid it, Daisy gingerly bit into a charred strip. It was so stiff it didn't budge. She tried a second bite, harder this time, and her teeth hurt from the effort. "Oh," she said, smiling with all her might. "It's very crispy. Super crispy."

"I'm glad you like it!" Piper turned her attention to Smitty, allowing Daisy the opportunity to subtly hit her bacon against the table in an effort to break a piece off.

"I know pancakes are your favorite, Smitty. Dig in!"

"Thanks." Smitty poked at the lumpy ball on his plate, but the pancake-ball slid away. He tried again with the same effect.

"Take a bite," Conrad hissed at him.

"I'm trying to," Smitty hissed back. "Have you seen this thing?" With his X-ray vision, Smitty sure had. "It's got the chemical composition of a rubber ball."

"Just stick it in your mouth and chew it."

Smitty stabbed the pancake-ball with murderous

intent, but the ball would not submit and instead shot off his plate and right at Joe, who had finally gathered the courage to take a sip of his coffee-mud. Just as the mud was sliding over his lips, Smitty's pancake-ball smacked into his cup, cracking it.

The coffee-mud exploded outward, splattering everyone.

At the same moment, Daisy whacked her bacon against the table with all her might (which for Daisy was considerable). The old table split in two with a CRACK!

The table collapsed inward, plates of food sliding off in all directions, projecting pancake-balls around the kitchen like atomic shrapnel.

"Take cover!"

A pancake-ball hit little Violet between the eyes, and she fell to the floor, out cold.

It was at that moment that the stove went up in flames.

"Oh no. I forgot the muffins!" Piper wailed.

Had there not been ten children with exceptional abilities on hand who had undergone years of emergency training, the McCloud farm would have burned to the ground that day. As it was, Joe set to work later that afternoon to make a new kitchen table, Betty ordered a new stove on the internet (with Conrad's help), and

Piper spent the rest of the day on her hands and knees scrubbing up the mess.

That night, for the first time ever, a pizza delivery boy showed up at the McCloud farm. He was instantly set upon by eleven half-starved children, prompting him to quit his job, go back to school, and become a doctor like his mother had always told him to do.

CHAPTER

14

*B*ETTY DECIDED AFTER THE KITCHEN incident that Piper should help out a little less, and definitely not in the kitchen. As Joe had the farm-work squared away, Betty sent Piper out to tend to the chickens and collect eggs. By mid-morning Piper was at loose ends again, and the other kids had gone off some-where Piper couldn't find them.

Stepping out onto the porch, Piper used her hand as a shield over her eyes and scanned the yard and the fields. Except for the cows and sheep, there wasn't a soul in sight.

What now?

The kids were probably working hard in the barn, Piper decided. Maybe she could help. She opened the door to the barn and stepped inside.

It was empty.

In the loft above, Conrad's various experiments

bubbled and fizzed. The meeting table was unoccupied and waiting. Piper walked up to the chair at the far end—her chair. She sat down in it and swiveled back and forth. At the other end of the table, facing her, sat Conrad's empty chair.

A scratching sound caught Piper's attention.

Searching about, Piper soon found Fido scratching at the door to the cellar.

"What's up, Fido?"

Fido paddled his paws against the door. He wanted out.

Piper opened the door, and Fido flew down the stairs. "Glad I can be of help to at least someone."

She was just about to close the door when she heard the muffled sound of voices. Cocking her ear, she stood very still and listened—yes, she definitely heard something.

Back before the kids had shown up, there had been stalls in the cellar of the barn for the cows to have shelter and warmth in winter. It was a dark, cobwebby place then, filled with swallows' nests, fallen hayseeds, manure, and the low, heavy smells of cows. Now the cows had a proper barn all their own with heated floors and automatic water troughs so that when they were thirsty, the water was always fresh. Coupled with good ventilation and lots of light, the cows were very happy in their new quarters, and the children had refurbished the cellar into snug bedrooms with a large storage area at the very back.

Creeping quietly down the stairs, Piper was led by the sounds she heard past the bedrooms to the door of the storage room. The door was ajar.

There was a light coming from the deepest part. Piper threaded her way through the boxes, and the closer she came to the light, the more the voices became familiar.

"I don't understand," someone said. It sounded like Jasper.

"When the bugs fly upward, they aren't going away," said a voice Piper knew better than her own: Conrad. She wedged herself into a hollow against a box, where she was hidden but could see what was happening.

From her vantage, she could make out all the kids. They were sitting on boxes, with Conrad in the middle. He'd set up his 3-D computer so that it was projected in the air and could be seen from all sides and was currently showing the way the bugs were burrowing out of the soil.

"Each bug's pattern is always the same. They climb out of the earth and wait for directional information. I believe they are communicating this to each other on a sonic frequency. Once they receive coordinates, they fly up and into position.

"This is what we're dealing with now." Conrad

activated a different view showing the earth from outer space and how it was surrounded by the large bugs. The bugs hovered at very specific intervals around the entire planet, like they were forming a net. "By my calculations, we can expect the entire planet to be surrounded by them in less than seven days."

"And what then?" Kimber half raised her hand. "What are they going to do?"

Conrad selected one of the bugs by tapping on its image and enlarged it. "Each bug has an energy sack where they are brewing a type of electromagnetic cocktail. When their bellies strobe red, they are preparing to blast it out, and when they do that, it creates a wave—a wall, if you will—of disruption."

"Exactly." Smitty jumped in at this point, getting to his feet. "It looks like an electromagnetic firestorm. These bugs have the power to wipe out anything that depends on magnets and technology." Smitty exploded his fist outward. "Poof. Gone. Just like that."

"So what?" Nalen shrugged, unimpressed. "Big deal. A few computers go down. That's what tech support is for. Next."

"One bug is not a big deal, but ten thousand bugs is a big deal," Conrad pointed out. "One hundred thousand is a whole new category. And you have to factor in the effect of all of them blasting synchronously.

In that eventuality the force of their blast will grow exponentially."

Conrad toggled his model to demonstrate. "If one bug looks like this . . ." Conrad showed a bug sending out a blast. "Then this is what it looks like when the planet is surrounded by them, and they all blast at the same time."

The bugs threw off a red explosion, showering the earth in an electromagnetic firestorm.

In unison, Nalen and Ahmed whistled low. "Chaos," Nalen said.

"Armageddon," Ahmed agreed.

"Exactly." Conrad nodded. "Every computer chip, cell phone, generator, solar panel; every satellite, motherboard—anything electronic will be wiped out. We rely on technology for everything, and once the computers go down on a scale of this size, the planet will be thrown back into the Dark Ages."

"Max probably liked the Dark Ages," Smitty said wryly. "It was easier for him to cause problems when he couldn't be tracked or watched."

"I'm so sick of Max and all his evil plans."

"You can say that again."

"So how do we stop it?"

Conrad took a deep breath. "That's the problem. If there were a hundred of them, we could do it. A thousand would even be possible, but with over one hundred

thousand, coming from every corner of the planet . . ."
He shook his head.

"How much time do we have?" Jasper asked, worried.

"I project one week. At most." Conrad paced.

"So what do we do?"

"We can't do it alone. We need help," Conrad said.
"We'll go to Xanthia."

Piper gasped.

Xanthia was a paradise populated by people who
all had exceptional abilities. They had chosen to hide
themselves away from the rest of the world and live in
peace and isolation. They called themselves the Chosen
Ones and refused to have anything to do with anyone
from the outside world, whom they called Outsiders.
Piper and Conrad had managed to get into their world
and learn about them, but they had refused to return to
the outside with Piper and her friends.

"If the Chosen Ones will combine their knowledge,
talents, and abilities with ours, there is a chance we can
stop this infestation and save the planet."

Kimber didn't have a high opinion of the altruis-
tic motives of the Chosen Ones, and she crossed her
arms over her chest. "What makes you think they'll
help us?"

"Because the survival of the planet depends upon it,
and they are living on the planet too." Conrad's voice

lacked conviction. "We'll move out first thing tomorrow morning."

There was a rustling as kids got to their feet. Piper shrunk back into a shadow, crouching out of sight.

"We'll need to travel light," Conrad said to the kids, who were already hustling out. "Gather up what you need and be ready at dawn. And, guys . . ."

There was a pause in the activity as they waited on Conrad's final words.

"We don't talk about this mission to anyone. All of this information is strictly between us."

A few of the kids muttered, but Kimber spoke up. "What you mean is that you don't want us to talk about it to Piper. This doesn't feel right, Conrad."

"Yeah," agreed Myrtle. "What are we gonna do? Sneak out in the morning?"

"Leave that to me." Conrad's voice was firm. "We can't risk having her with us. Piper stays behind."

It felt to Piper that she was going to ignite or explode. She cringed for the shame of it all. Her friends hadn't been busy—they had been purposely leaving her out. They were now having secret meetings just so that she wouldn't find out.

The thought of them leaving without her—of being left behind—was unbearable. She wouldn't, she couldn't let that happen.

Piper was careful to remain absolutely still and not make a sound until the meeting was over. It didn't take long, because the others were anxious to get going and had a lot to do before they left. When it was safe to go, Piper snuck out to make her own plans.

CHAPTER

15

*P*IPER DECIDED TO JUMP OFF THE ROOF of her house.

This was her plan: shimmy out her window, mount the ridgepole, pick up speed by running from one end all the way to the other. Then jump off.

The first time Piper had flown, this is what she had done. It only stood to reason that it would work on her second attempt.

Piper lifted the window to her bedroom slowly so that it didn't make a sound. Three equally silent maneuvers later, she was outside on the roof. She'd been on the roof so often that the feeling of the shingles on her feet was as familiar to her as the braided rug on her bedroom floor.

Still, she hadn't climbed the shingles in a while. There was little reason for her to do that when she could just fly. She climbed slowly now, soundlessly and carefully, focusing on the way she placed her feet and, at times, bending over to steady herself with her hands. When she got to the top, she stood up straight.

The first time she'd jumped off the roof she'd been scared too. Not quite as scared as she was at that moment, but near enough. And it wasn't just fear this time; it was desperation. The feeling that she *had* to fly: that without flying, she couldn't go on.

It was still quite dark.

Maybe she should wait?

No, best to go quickly.

Raising her arms to shoulder height, Piper took a deep breath and started. One step, two steps. She picked up speed.

"Stop!"

Startled, Piper lost her balance, stumbling.

Conrad rushed up the side of the roof and grabbed hold of her arm just as she was about to tumble down the other side. When she'd regained her balance, they both crouched close to the roof.

"What are you doing out here?" Piper pushed Conrad's hand away.

Conrad's face was as white as a sheet. "I could ask you the same question."

"I'm—None of your business."

"You came up here to jump. I know what you are

thinking, Piper, but if you fall off this roof, you'll kill yourself."

"Jasper would have healed me if I fell."

"Jasper can't heal dead," Conrad argued. "There are limits—for all of us."

"I wasn't going to die, and maybe, just maybe, I could have—"

"Flown." Conrad finished her thought and then shook his head.

Color rose in Piper's face. "The last time I jumped off the roof, I did fly. Maybe I just need to try again. You don't know!"

"I do know, Piper, because we've tried everything. If you still had the ability to fly, then you'd have done it."

Piper pulled her lips into a hard line. "I'm going to jump. I can fly. It's my choice."

Conrad got quiet and placed his hand across his mouth, thinking before he spoke. "I was going to tell you before, but I wanted proof. The truth is, Piper, that you aren't like us anymore."

Piper was aware that this moment was somehow very important. It made time wrap around itself and slow down. She released her breath in a measured way before she allowed herself to speak.

"What do you mean?"

"I took blood samples from all of us, the entire team,"

Conrad explained. "All of us have an extra hybrid gene between our thirty-third and thirty-fourth chromosomes." Conrad cupped his hands. "It's unprecedented. I've never seen anything like it." For a moment the scientific novelty of his discovery converted Conrad's face from sad to excited. "I believe that extra chromosome is the reason that we can do the things we do. It's like a switch or a conductor inside us that lets us be who we are. I call it the superhero cell."

"And we all have it? The same thing?"

"Yes! We all do." Conrad pointed to himself when he said "we" but not at Piper. "I went back to the stored DNA samples from before, and you had it too. Except not now."

"You mean it's gone? Just disappeared?"

Conrad nodded.

"Well, find a way to put it back in so I can go back to the way I was!" Piper had seen Conrad do so many amazing things, surely this wouldn't be difficult for him to fix.

Conrad shook his head. "When the bug bit you, the venom reprogrammed your immune system to reject the superhero cell. Even if I transplant one from your stored DNA and replace it in your body, your immune system will attack it and kill it."

"So get me a new immune system. Change my DNA!" Piper felt herself getting frustrated.

"I can't fix it, Piper. There's no way for me to get you a new immune system and change your DNA."

"If you wanted to, you could."

"You know that's not true."

Piper could feel her frustration bubbling and popping. She felt like a teakettle at full boil. "Maybe you like the fact I can't fly."

"That doesn't even make sense, Piper." The sun was pushing over the horizon, and Conrad was aware that the others would be gathered and waiting for him. They had a long way to travel to get to Xanthia and time was of the essence. He got up and started down the roof. "We'll talk about this when I get back."

"No." Piper jumped to her feet and stood on the ridgepole. "I want to come with you to Xanthia. I'm part of the team too, and I want to help."

Conrad stopped. "You know you can't come."

"Why not? Because you don't want me to?"

"Piper, they'll never let you into Xanthia as you are now. Last time was different—you could fly then. You know how the Chosen Ones are about Outsiders and people who aren't extraordinary."

A wild river of rage burst Piper's dams. Her body

started to shake from the force of it. "*You* don't want me. That's the problem. If you wanted to help me, you would. You like going around feeling superior to me and leaving me out, not telling me things, treating me like I'm a stranger." Piper stamped her foot. "You aren't very nice, Conrad. This is my house. All of this was my idea. I was the one who invited you here. You just treat me like . . . dirt."

Conrad's face was now flushing with anger. "No one is treating you like dirt. I have done everything I could—"

"Everything but help me to fly. You just wanted me out of the way because I'm inconvenient."

Hurt shone in Conrad's blue eyes. "That's the most unkind, mean thing you've ever said, Piper McCloud." He dragged his hand through his hair, pulling it from his face. They had been friends for a long time, and they'd had their squabbles and their differences of opinions, often on a daily basis, but they'd never truly fought, and never ugly like this.

Piper's fingers curled into fists. The fact that Conrad was attempting to be calm and rational only served to infuriate her more. "I will not go to the dance with you," she said.

Conrad formed several questions and released them before he uttered, "What dance?"

"The spring dance!" Piper shook her head at his obtuseness. "I know you didn't ask me, but even if you did ask, I wouldn't go with you. So don't ask. The answer is no."

Conrad was on the verge of unraveling the mystery of this remark when he thought the better of it. "I have to go."

Conrad walked down the roof.

Piper stood up on the ridgepole, pulling her arms out to her side and preparing to run.

"Don't do it, Piper." Conrad didn't turn around.

"I can fly."

"No, you can't fly, and you have to accept that. You have to get on with your life."

Piper snorted. "Without flying? Impossible."

"Being extraordinary has its perks. You know that as well as I do, but it's not what makes us great, and it's not everything," Conrad said, glancing back at her. "There are other things you can do . . ."

"What other things?"

"We'll talk about it when I come back." Conrad slipped through the window and was gone.

Standing alone on the roof, Piper was faced with a decision: either take her chances and jump, or get off the roof and find a way to be normal.

Piper could hear the team below wordlessly loading

into the transport. Soon after, they moved out, and the farm was quiet again.

The sun came over the horizon, and the dawn turned to morning. When the rooster crowed, Piper sat down, defeated.

"Pa? Pa! PA!"

Joe McCloud rushed out of the kitchen door, clutching his shotgun in one hand and the tops of his still-undone overalls in the other.

"I'm up here, Pa."

Joe looked up. When he spotted Piper sitting slumped over on the roof, his face became confused.

Tears of shame prickled Piper's eyes. "I can't get down, Pa. Can you help me? I think I need a ladder."

Joe put his shotgun down and scratched his head but then fetched the long ladder from the toolshed. When it was safely up against the side of the house, he helped Piper climb down. He helped her to the ground, and it was only then that she felt that her legs were shaking.

"Thanks, Pa. I won't ever go up there again." Piper walked in the house and shut the door behind her.

CHAPTER

16

*I*T HAD BEEN FIVE HOURS AND TWENTY-three minutes since Conrad had told Piper she was normal.

Five long hours. Twenty-three excruciating minutes.

Did time move more slowly for normal people? She wondered if she would be able to make it to lunch.

The first thing Piper did after she returned to the house was set about cleaning her room. Her room was not large; none of the rooms in the McCloud house could be described as spacious. It consisted of a single bed, on top of which lay a quilt with patches of pink and green and blue. Her bed frame had been hand carved by Joe, and Piper used a cloth to follow the flowing lines of the wood and clean dust away from the details. She took the braided rug that sat at the foot of her bed and shook it out and then set about organizing her small bookshelf. She removed all the books and stacked them on the floor. After she carefully dusted them, she replaced them on the shelves. She decided to rearrange the books, first sorting them from largest to smallest and then changing her mind and sorting them by color instead.

Piper had a small wardrobe consisting of T-shirts and jeans and three dresses. The dresses had not had a lot of use and were already on the small side. She took all six pairs of jeans she owned and refolded them neatly. In a stack next to them she placed her T-shirts—three red, one orange, and two blue. She lined her shoes up in a straight row and placed the dresses precisely on each hanger, leaving exactly two inches between them so that the closet would have symmetry.

The only thing left in the room was her desk, and when Piper sat down at it, she found her scrapbook on the top in a jumble. She'd been working on it off and on for years, but there had never been enough time to finish. In the past, no sooner would she sit down and start to work on it than Max would get up to no good, and off the team would go to save the world again. Obviously, there was no danger of that happening today, so Piper allowed herself the luxury of looking carefully at all her mementos.

The kids had been together for several years, and in the early pictures Piper could see when she'd lost a tooth or how short her hair was or how Jasper and Lily, who were the youngest, had grown. There was a picture of her and Jasper at the Eiffel Tower, their arms thrown around each other and grins on their faces. That was taken after they had thwarted Max's plans to blow up a metro station. And here a picture of Lily, Myrtle, Daisy, and Violet laughing and eating gelato in Rome. In page after page Piper was reminded of the good that they had done, the trouble they had overcome, the power of their friendships.

On the very last page was a picture of her with Conrad. They were relaxed, happy, victorious. The photo had been taken on a good day; they'd pulled two hundred earthquake victims trapped in the basement of a building to safety. Without Piper flying up and down, lifting each one through a narrow opening, it wouldn't have happened. Conrad had warned her to be careful, because the structure was unstable and could collapse at any moment. Piper had gone ahead and done it anyway, and at the end of the day, Conrad had told her that they couldn't have saved all those people without her. Those were his words.

"We couldn't have done it without you, Piper," Conrad said.

"You couldn't have done it without me," Piper whispered, running her hand over the photograph.

When she'd positioned the last photo and everything was in order, Piper placed the scrapbook in a position of honor on her bookshelf and stood in the center of her room.

Piper felt the silence and stillness. It didn't feel good. She looked at the clock—all that cleaning and organizing had only taken her ninety minutes, and now it was done. How many more normal minutes did that leave for her to fill?

Gingerly sitting on her bed, Piper looked at the wall. She sat like that for a while until she noticed that her breath caught in her throat on the way in, and her vision was blurry.

———◆———

PIPER DECIDED TO COLLECT EGGS IN THE henhouse, and as she did so, she attempted to wrap her mind around what she would do with the thousands and thousands of normal hours that stretched before her.

Fido perched on the window of the henhouse and listened as a good friend should (but mainly watched the eggs in the hopes that one might come his way).

"What do other kids do with themselves?" Piper asked Fido. For almost four years her main focus had been saving the planet from an evil kid bent on world domination. It hadn't left her much time for hobbies.

Fido snarfled.

"Maybe I'm a sporty girl. What do you think? Soccer?" Piper imagined kicking a black-and-white ball around and getting excited when her team scored a goal.

"Go, team!" she cheered. That felt awkward. It was one thing to get excited when you stopped a train from falling off a bridge, but the excitement she could muster for a ball going into a net was limited.

"I'm probably more of a theater kid." Piper struck a pose. "Hark, what light shines from yonder window?"

Fido let fly a loud, wet sneeze.

"Or I could get an iPad and download apps." Would she sit in the barn and play her apps while the other kids were saving the world around her? That didn't feel right, either. Piper bent down to reach for an egg that had rolled away and gathered it up when she noticed another egg that had been tucked back behind some straw. Sometimes the chickens hid eggs away, and it wasn't always easy to find them all. There was no telling how long ago this egg had been laid. Reaching for the egg, Piper noticed it was cracked. Not only that, but the inhabitant of the egg was trying to get out.

"Oh," Piper said in shock. She watched as a little beak pecked and pecked at the shell. She found herself rooting for the little chick inside. "C'mon, you can do it," she coached. The baby chick had managed to create a hole but wasn't strong enough to break out.

"Let me help you, little guy," Piper cooed. Very gently she took her finger and broke open the egg, placing it on the straw. The chick lay in the half shell, its chest heaving.

Piper's face smiled at the miracle of the little life in front of her. She blew a gentle, warm breeze on the chick to dry it off and give it comfort.

"See that, Fido? We've got a new friend."

Fido barked.

"No, you leave it alone and let it get strong. It'll be fine once it's had a chance to catch its breath."

Hunkering down in the straw, Piper took the time to watch as the chick enjoyed its first moments of life. Maybe life wasn't going to be so bad after all, she decided.

A scream came from the house. Piper stopped what she was doing to listen when a second cry hit the breeze. Dropping the eggs, Piper ran as fast as her legs would carry her through the yard, onto the porch, and past the screen door.

"Ma?"

Piper discovered Betty doubled over, her arms on the kitchen counter, her head resting on her arms.

"Ma?"

"Ohhh," Betty moaned. "I got me a wicked bellyache."

"I'll run for Doc Bell." Piper was already halfway out the door.

"No, no; go fetch your pa. Hurry now."

Piper ran like the wind. Joe was fixing the fence on the far end of the north pasture, and when she got to him, she could hardly get the words out. "Ma—stomach—doctor."

Joe dropped what he was doing, and the two of them rushed back to the house. While Piper helped her mother, Joe brought the pickup truck around, and together they made the short trip into town with as much speed as the old truck could manage. It was the middle of the day, and Doc Bell's waiting room was chockablock full of patients. One look at Betty's face, and Dottie Dutton, the receptionist, whisked her into the examining room.

"You best go back to the waiting room, Piper, and I'll fetch you when you're needed," Doc Bell said when he saw the state Betty was in.

"Is Ma gonna be okay? Let me help you . . ."

"Dottie, take Piper out front, and you'll have to tell the others that they best come back tomorrow."

"Oh dear. Oh no. This is terrible," Mrs. Dutton said, pulling Piper out the door.

Dottie Dutton had worked for Doc Bell since he started in Lowland County and had helped out Doc Archibald before him, and during her tenure she had become impossibly old. She'd seen everything that could go wrong to a soul go wrong, and instead of being inoculated against tragedy had remained steadfastly shocked and alarmed by any new medical emergency—even ones she'd seen before or weren't particularly serious. Needless to say, this was not a good quality for a medical receptionist to have.

In a state of near hyperventilation, Dottie Dutton sat Piper down in the waiting room.

"Go home!" Mrs. Dutton told the other waiting patients. "Doc Bell won't see you today, so shoo. Come back tomorrow if you must. Now, git."

After the confused patients were pushed out the door, Dottie opened a package of peppermints. Her hands were shaking so much she dropped several on the floor before she managed to shove one in her mouth and then suck on it loudly, like she couldn't stop herself, like the peppermint was the only thing that was keeping her sane.

"Oh my, oh my," she said, listening to Betty's moans. "That doesn't sound good. It surely doesn't."

Piper's hands clutched each other in a death grip. "She'll be okay, though."

"You must prepare yourself." Dottie Dutton shook her head sadly. Tears gathered in Dottie's eyes, and she dabbed at them.

The walls in Doc Bell's offices must have been made of paper, because every moan and cry Betty made was heard plain as day in the waiting room. Piper took to holding her breath for as long as they lasted. Dottie Dutton, on the other hand, clutched her throat like she couldn't breathe or covered the shotgun gasps that ejected from her throat by stuffing a handkerchief into her mouth and finally put her head down on the desk altogether and smothered it with her arms like the world itself was coming to an end.

"I can't take it," Dottie whimpered. "This is the worst thing that's ever happened."

Piper put her hands over her ears and pressed as hard as she was able.

In the midst of this, the door to the waiting room flew open with a crash, and there stood Jimmy Joe Miller, dramatically holding one foot up in the air out in front of him. The foot was without a sock or shoe, and the big toe was smashed up such that blood was shooting out of it.

Dottie Dutton leapt to her feet and screamed at the top of her lungs.

Jimmy Joe was extremely pleased with this reception,

and he hopped in, spewing blood as he went. "Got my foot smashed, and Ma says that Doc Bell needs to take a look."

Dottie's mouth opened and closed, strangled squeaking coming out of it. "I—you—Doc—Oh no! Oh no!"

"Dottie, git back here," Doc Bell called out from the examining room. "I need an extra pair of hands."

Dottie Dutton fled.

Jimmy Joe Miller hobbled in, eyeing Piper.

"What you lookin' at?" Jimmy Joe snapped.

"Nothing," Piper said pointedly.

"You calling me nothing?"

A sharp moan from the examining room made Piper flinch. Jimmy Joe snorted and rolled his eyes. "That your ma in there making all that racket?"

"Shut your piehole, Jimmy Joe Miller," Piper blazed. She wasn't going to have a Miller making fun of her ma at a time like this.

Normally, Jimmy Joe, sensing weakness, went in for the kill, but the way Piper was fixed to her seat like a dangling icicle ready to shatter off, it didn't seem like there was any sport to it.

"My pa fell off the barn roof in spring. He smacked himself up good, and he was moaning something awful too. He made a noise that sounded like a bear wrestling

with a mountain lion." Jimmy Joe attempted to demonstrate what that sounded like.

"ArggggghhhhHHHHHmmm."

Thinking about a bear wrestling with a mountain
lion, as well as enduring Jimmy Joe's vocal gyrations,
took Piper's mind off her mother, and for this she was
grateful. By this point, a small pool of blood was col-
lecting on the floor, so Piper got up and helped Jimmy
Joe to a chair.

"Here," she said, getting him settled.

"I fell from the top of the rafters and my foot hit the
side of the hay bailer and my boot got torn in two. Then
blood started shooting out of my toe. It's a gusher, huh?
Bet you never seen this much blood!"

Piper swung another chair around, put it in front of
Jimmy Joe, and lifted his leg up so that the hurt toe was
elevated. "It's a lotta blood."

"It hurts like all hellfire, too." This seemed to please
him.

Piper took off the handkerchief around her neck and
put it on the toe, applying pressure.

"DARN IT—that stings!"

Piper couldn't help but notice that Jimmy Joe's foot
was filthy. Somehow the filth on his foot was a comfort
to her. It was just like the red spots on her body and

the sickness that had taken hold of her ma; part of the indignity of being flesh and blood and how your body betrays you. They were none of them immune to it.

"Guess you never fell down like this," Jimmy Joe smirked, "being the way you are."

"What way is that?"

"Weird. Strange. You and your freak friends. All the weird things y'all do." Jimmy Joe looked out the window, expecting to see them outside. "Where they at, anyway?"

"They had something to do."

"Oh yeah. So why ain't you doing it with them?"

Piper shrugged. "I'm not like them anymore."

"Yeah, right."

"It's true."

"You never was right in the head, Piper McCloud. No one believes a word that comes out of your mouth."

There she was being nice to him, and still he was saying mean things to her. Just like a Miller too! "I'm glad you hurt your toe," Piper flashed, getting up. "You deserved it."

"Anyone tell you that those red spots on your face make you look diseased?"

Piper went to the chair as far from Jimmy Joe as she could get and plunked down on it, crossing her arms over her chest. "I sure hope Doc Bell's not gonna have to cut that toe off."

"Oh, I'll be right as rain," Jimmy Joe smirked. "Not like your ma. She sounds like she's a goner, if you ask me."

As Piper sat seething, she realized it had gotten very quiet—too quiet. The quiet was worse than the noise.

After Piper endured a few minutes of the miserable silence, Dottie Dutton slipped back into the waiting room and sat down at her desk in a daze. "I'm only supposed to keep the reception desk," she said. "It's all I'm trained for."

Piper got to her feet. "Mrs. Dutton, ma'am, is my ma . . ."

Doris looked up, remembering that she had two people in the waiting room. "Oh, yes, Piper. Doc Bell says that you should go in now."

Piper gulped. "Is my ma gonna be okay?"

"Your life won't never be the same after today, child," she said ominously. "Go on in, now. Go on."

Piper took one careful step followed by another to the door. Her hand rested on the doorknob for longer than it needed to before she turned it. There was a short hallway that led to the examining room, and when she reached the final door, she knocked softly. The exam room door was instantly thrust open.

"Well, well," Doc Bell beamed. "Congratulations, young lady."

Doc Bell stepped aside, allowing Piper a view of the room. There, in front of her, was her mother, holding a little baby swaddled up tightly. Joe was standing at Betty's side, and he looked like Piper felt: confused, terrified . . . with a dawning sense of elation.

"You, Piper McCloud, are officially a big sister," Doc Bell announced.

CHAPTER

17

*P*IPER COULD NOT UNDERSTAND THE meaning of Doc Bell's words. Of course she understood the words themselves, but the way he'd put them together didn't make any sense at all to her. "I'm a what?"

"Your ma just had a baby, Piper." Doc Bell beamed. "You're a big sister now."

Piper turned to her mother. "Ma? Are you alright?"

"Your ma'll be just fine." Doc Bell patted Piper's shoulders.

Piper let out a strangled laugh that sounded like a sob.

"Calm yourself, child." Betty's voice was tired but happy.

A loud slamming could be heard coming from the waiting room. "Where is Doc Bell, I'd like to know?" It was the sharp, high voice of Millie Mae Miller. "How come my boy's out here bleeding to death?"

Doc Bell shook his head and gathered up a small tray of supplies. "Excuse me, folks."

Piper tried to come to terms with the new circumstances of her life. "But . . . but I didn't know you was having a baby."

"You ain't the only one who's surprised," Betty admitted. "Just thought I was feeling a bit tired. Guess I wasn't paying attention." Betty offered the bundle of baby to Piper. "Here."

"Me?" Piper received the baby into trembling arms.

"She's a girl."

"A girl? You're a little girl!" Piper cooed. The baby was strangely compact but heavy. Her hands were grasping and opening, reaching out to life. She grabbed Piper's braid and pulled on it. Piper nearly melted on the spot. "Oh. She's so strong."

"Your pa and I are thinking of calling her Jane. Jane McCloud. Plain and simple and nothing fancy."

"Jane," Piper repeated.

Dottie Dutton came bustling into the room with an envelope that she handed to Joe. "Doc Bell had me call ahead, and they're expecting you down at the hospital in Cloverfield. Here's all the information they'll need."

"The hospital?" Piper's head jerked up. "Why the hospital?"

"I'm fine, child. Don't get that look on your face. They just need to check things out."

Dottie Dutton made a tsking noise as she packed up Betty's chart. "You should always prepare yourself for the worst."

With those happy words, Dottie bustled out of the room, leaving the door open so that Millie Mae could come bursting in. She presented herself at the foot of the examining table like she'd happened upon a party that she should have gotten an invitation to but hadn't. Placing her hands on her hips, she surveyed the scene with contempt.

"Well, you could knock me over with a feather, Betty McCloud," she sniffed. "Dottie Dutton just told me what you got up to in here, and I couldn't believe it if I didn't see it with my own eyes. What were you thinking, going off and having another baby for? And at your age too?" Millie Mae swooped forward and plucked the baby out of Piper's hands before she could protest.

"Well, this one don't look strange. Not like what you got now. That's a blessing anyway." Mille Mae looked closer. "She don't have the color I like to see in a newborn, though. Had six of my own, so I know about these things."

Betty reached out to the baby anxiously. "We're going off to the hospital in Cloverfield, and she'll be checked out good."

"Just as well. You can't be too careful. No telling what can go wrong when a woman of your age goes around having babies unexpected-like." Millie Mae shrugged as though to say that Betty deserved what she got for what was an obvious lack of common sense.

"Your boy has a nasty cut," Doc Bell said, bumbling back into the room with Dottie Dutton at his side. "Nothing much wrong with him besides. I bandaged it up so that it'll hold the night, but you best bring him back first thing in the morning so I can take another look at it."

This came as no surprise to Millie Mae. "I suspected as much."

All business, Doc Bell scooped the baby out of Betty's arms and handed her to Joe. With Dottie Dutton on one side of Betty and him on the other, they began to hoist her off the examining table. "We'll need to get you loaded up and on the road over to Cloverfield. They're expecting you before night, and it's a long drive. Best get a move on."

Piper wanted to help her mother, but there were too many people, and she was pushed aside and out of the way.

"Careful, now," Millie Mae clucked. "For heaven's sake, don't drop her."

In no time flat, Betty was loaded up into the back of Doc Bell's large station wagon, and Joe and the baby were settled into the backseat. Piper ran around to the passenger side and grabbed hold of the door to get in.

"Well, heavens sake, where do you think you're going?" Millie Mae spat, eyeing Piper. "They don't want you cluttering up the hospital, and your parents don't got time for you now that they got this brand-new baby."

Piper's mouth fell open. "But . . ."

"Hospitals are no place for a youngen," Doc Bell agreed.

"She's not old enough to stay by herself at the farm. There's no telling what she'll get up to," Betty called out from the back of the station wagon.

Piper's cheeks colored up. The Stark Raven incident was obviously still fresh in Betty's mind. "I'll be fine, Ma. I won't get up to trouble."

"I won't be able to rest at the hospital for worrying about you. Millie Mae's right." It was a rare occasion for Betty and Millie Mae to be on the same page. "Thanks for offering to look after her, Millie Mae."

Millie Mae's mouth flew open. "I never—"

Doc Bell started the engine.

"I expect you to be on your best behavior, Piper McCloud," Betty called out as the car started to pull away.

"But, Ma . . ."

"Promise me you'll do your best to fit in, Piper."

Doc Bell stepped on the gas, and the old station wagon rocketed down the dirt road, leaving Piper and Millie Mae in a cloud of dust.

Millie Mae opened and closed her mouth several times trying to get over the shock of what had just happened. "I never said no such thing! I never!" Millie Mae clucked to herself. "I think having that baby addled your mama's brain and she was hearing things that weren't said."

"Yes, ma'am!" A temporary case of insanity on her mama's part was the only explanation Piper could think of as to why she was suddenly in the custody of Millie Mae Miller. The whole situation was inexplicable! Not to mention horrifying.

Millie Mae turned on Piper like it was her fault. "I don't take any nonsense from youngens. You best watch yourself and mind you don't get my temper riled."

Millie Mae turned on her heel to fetch Jimmy Joe.

Piper stood like a statue, watching Millie Mae walk away. She considered disobeying her mother, running away, walking to the hospital in Cloverfield, or anything that didn't involve going with Millie Mae and staying at the Miller house. Anything.

"Well, c'mon," Millie Mae snapped irritably. "I don't got all day."

Pursing her lips, Piper held her breath and followed after Millie Mae like a dog with its tail between its legs.

CHAPTER

18

"THERE'S NO POINT SHOWING YOU around, 'cause you won't be here long enough to get settled" was the first thing out of Millie Mae's lips when they returned to the Miller farm. "Still and all, since you're here, you might as well make yourself useful."

With that, Millie Mae draped Piper in a frilly apron covered with impossibly large flowers, sealed her into it with a tight bow at the back, sat her down with a bag of potatoes, and ordered her to start peeling.

Even though Piper had lived a stone's throw away her whole life, this was the first time she had ever actually set foot on the Miller property. The house was a perfect square, made of solid stone, and sported flower boxes on each window with fluttering lace curtains. There was a pretense of orderliness that was successfully upheld from a distance, but upon closer inspection, it was clear to

Piper that the entire place was one dirty sock away from absolute chaos. With five active boys between the ages of thirteen (Jimmy Joe) and eighteen (Rory Ray), things were bursting at the seams. Millie Mae was fastidious by nature, but the woman was clearly overwhelmed by the baseball bats, pinewood boxcars, roller skates, hockey sticks, and dirty socks—mainly it was the dirty, stinky socks.

When they'd first driven up the driveway, they came upon the boys beating each other over the head with sticks and hollering at the top of their lungs. Millie Mae effectively put a stop to that by snatching up their sticks and beating them over their heads while hollering at the top of her lungs to "quit acting like numbskulls."

Next they discovered Sally Sue skulking in the house, gently crying over her most precious doll, which the boys had used for target practice. She held the limp doll in her hand, pointing to the holes and tears in her. Millie Mae took up the injured friend and tossed her in the trash.

"Boys will be boys, Sally Sue," Millie Mae said. "You know that. It's up to you to take better care of your things."

"But, Ma," Sally Sue wailed, her eyes erupting in real fountains of tears now, "they're stronger than I am, and they just held me down and took her . . ." And the tears overtook Sally Sue altogether, and Millie Mae put a potato peeler into her hand and put her to work too.

"I'm sorry about your doll, Sally Sue," Piper offered quietly when they were well into the mound of potatoes and Sally Sue's tears had remained steady.

"She was my best one," Sally Sue mourned. "I told her all my secrets. I don't have no one else."

Before, when Piper had only been able to float and her parents had kept her home alone, she had gazed at the Miller children's daily trek past her farm to school with longing. In her fantasies she had settled upon Sally Sue as her best friend and had imagined their lifelong friendship together. Piper had lots of friends now, or at least she used to. She didn't have any normal friends, though.

"You can talk to me," Piper said.

"You?"

"Why not? I don't live that far away," Piper pointed out. "We're the same age, and I'd listen; I'd understand."

Sally Sue's face snapped into an expression other than grief, and it looked suspiciously like shock. "Me come see you? At your farm? But you're . . ." She didn't use the words "strange," "weird," "freak," but her lips formed each one before she finally gave up and said, "I don't think I could do that, Piper. My pa would never let me. You know that."

Piper did know. She knew it in the same way that she knew that no one would ever sit next to her in church, even if there was standing room only. The same way she'd never come calling to the Miller farm, even though she'd lived by it her whole life. The lines in Lowland County were not on the soil but in folks' hearts.

Piper had always been an optimist, though, and a great believer in change. "Well, I'm not the same as I was before," she said, "so maybe things can be different for us, too."

"Maybe," Sally Sue murmured halfheartedly.

After they'd finished the potatoes, there was corn to shuck, apples to slice, and the table to set. In the midst of their work, Bobby Boo and Jo-Jo James, the middle boys, took it into their heads to blow up the manure pile using a combination of Millie Mae's laundry detergent and baking powder. The manure pile was scattered for miles, and the boys were covered in dung. They celebrated this achievement by giving each other rousing high fives.

"Bobby Jo, you're a mess, and look at the mess you made," Millie Mae spat.

Bobby Boo and Jo-Jo James were born less than a year apart and spent all their time plotting and scheming, mainly with explosives. They were known within the family as Bobby Jo because it just saved time.

"I told you boys to stay outside and play quiet, and look at this." Millie Mae threw up her hands and then dispatched them to the pond to wash up and not come back until they didn't stink. Then she told Piper and Sally Sue off for idling around when there was work to be done and to get back in the house where they belonged.

Back in the kitchen Piper looked at the phone, willing it to ring with news of baby Jane.

"I got a new baby sister," she told Sally Sue. "Her name is Jane. Jane McCloud. I got to hold her, and she felt like . . ." Piper paused to put the feeling into words. "She felt better than flying."

"A *sister*!" Sally Sue said the word "sister" in the same voice she'd utter the words "cotton candy" or "ice cream" or "heaven."

"She's at the hospital with my ma, but they'll be fine. They'll be home tonight. Probably call and say they're coming to get me any minute." Piper looked back at the phone. "Or maybe they'll just stop by without calling. Could be any minute."

Piper looked out the window and waited and waited.

CHAPTER

19

To Piper's great disappointment, only one car came up the Miller driveway that day, and it belonged to Dick Miller, who had spent the day at the seed co-op over in Shankville. Dick Miller had the face of a boiled lobster and the body of a gnarled tree trunk.

As soon as she saw her husband, Millie Mae sounded the dinner bell, which brought a stampede of feet from every corner of the farm. In the midst of hand washing, Piper was instructed to carry bowls of steaming potatoes, corn, hot biscuits, and fried chicken to the table. There was jostling for seats and scraping of chairs, but when Dick Miller set himself down and bowed his head for grace, there wasn't a sound to be heard.

With the blessing out of the way, Piper grabbed a biscuit from the plate directly in front of her. It had been a long day, and she hadn't eaten in hours. It was

only when her mouth was full to bursting that she realized no one else was eating. Instead, every Miller was
looking at her with reproach.

Dick Miller's jaw clenched and unclenched as he
waited, his face growing ever redder. Piper painfully swallowed her mouthful of bread. "Sorry," she mumbled.

Mr. Miller did not accept her apology but burned
her with his silence. He picked up the plate of fried
chicken and stabbed the best pieces for himself, keeping
his eyes on Piper the whole time. Next, he handed the
plate to Rory Ray, who, likewise, took as much as he
wanted.

Piper watched as Mr. Miller went through dish after
dish. By the time Sally Sue was given the chicken plate,
only one measly piece remained. When all was said and
done, Piper's meal consisted of one potato and a table-
spoon of corn.

"What's that?" Mr. Miller flicked his head at "that"—
"that" being Piper.

"Oh, Dick, her ma went and had a baby today for no
good reason. They took her off to the hospital, and there
wasn't anyone else who could look after the youngen. I
didn't have no choice—I had to take her." Millie Mae
spoke quickly, as though anticipating a problem. "She'll
go home soon. Probably right after dinner they'll come
get her. Maybe before then."

"Don't need any of her hijinks around here."

"Oh there won't be no hijinks," Millie Mae sniffed. "She can't do that flying no more."

Dick's face screwed up. "What's that you say?"

"She grew out of it. She's no different than the rest of us now." Millie Mae bit off a large chunk of chicken, grease running out of the corners of her mouth. "That's why she ain't with them others now. They don't want her no more."

"Is that right?" Dick fixed Piper with a satisfied stare, his lips curling into a smug grin.

Piper's cheeks burned with a hot shame, and she lost what little appetite she had left. Mr. Miller grunted and ate his food like it was putting up a fight.

"Billy Bean over at the seed co-op had a head full of steam today," Dick Miller chuckled. "Came in telling a tall tale of a giant cockroach climbing out of his field. Said it was bigger than a bale of hay and louder than ten cows." Dick shook his head over the craziness of the story. "We told him we wanted to see it, but he says it flew away. We laughed ourselves silly. I tol' him, 'Cockroaches can't fly, you fool,' and he got madder than a wet hen. Claims he's got a hole the size of a wheelbarrow in his wheat field to prove it."

Millie Mae snorted like a pig. "Sounds to me like Billy Bean's been at his moonshine again."

"Ha!" Dick Miller pointed his fork at Millie Mae. "You got that right."

The two of them laughed and ate their chicken legs.

Piper cleared her throat. "Actually," she offered politely, "Billy Bean was mistaken on only one point: it's not a cockroach. It is a large bug, though, and it could have made a hole in his wheat field the size of a wheelbarrow. Bigger even."

"What's this?" Dick Miller put down his food and wiped his face in a rough, sweeping motion. "Who asked you?"

"No one," Piper admitted. "I just thought you'd want to know the truth—"

"I know what's true and what's fake, and there's no such thing as giant bugs coming out of wheat fields."

"She ain't right in the head, Dick. She probably can't understand what you're saying." Millie Mae sucked a chicken bone like a lollipop.

"While you're under my roof, I'll thank you to keep your lies to yourself," he said to Piper.

Piper opened her mouth, but Jimmy Joe, who was sitting across from her, gave her a good swift kick under the table. When she looked up at him, he had warning in his eye, and she shut her mouth. Sitting quietly, Piper watched the Miller family clean their plates.

"Pa," Rory Ray said tentatively, having waited for just the right opportunity. There were few better moments than when his father had a full belly. "That recruiter called again today. He said they got a spot open for me in training camp this summer if I sign up."

Rory Ray held out a shiny pamphlet. On the front it said MARINES, and it showed men in uniform, covered in muck, looking strong and brave.

Mr. Miller grabbed the pamphlet. "Marines! Ha! You think you got the smarts to be one of them?"

Rory Ray leaned forward, his eyes shining, his face flushed. "The recruiter said I'm a good candidate, and they're looking for men like me. He said—"

"Men? You ain't a man, boy. You dig those fence posts like I told you?"

"Well, Pa, I was . . ."

"Didn't think so. If you can't dig a fence post, how you gonna do this?" Mr. Miller crumpled the pamphlet and tossed it away. "Honest farmwork is all you need. We're not gonna talk about this again. You don't got it in you."

Rory Ray bit his lip and salvaged his Marine pamphlet from the chicken grease it had landed in. With great care he wiped it clean on his shirt and then folded it into his pocket.

Dick Miller leaned back in his chair and dared anyone else to make fool-headed requests. No one did.

The sharp ringing of the telephone in the hallway jolted every single person at the table. Piper jumped to her feet like she'd been shot.

Dick Miller's fist came down on the table, reestablishing order. "We don't answer the phone during dinner!" he thundered. "SIT DOWN!"

"But . . ." Piper pointed to the ringing phone, edging her body over to it. "My ma's in the hospital. The baby . . . They said they were going to call."

"Then they'll call back."

"Mr. Miller, please. My ma might need me."

Dick Miller got to his feet. "Maybe Joe McCloud don't know how to run his farm, but over here we do things different. You touch that phone, and you won't like what's coming your way."

Piper hesitated. The phone was so close; she was only a short reach away . . . If she could still fly, it would have been no effort at all.

Ring. Ring. Ring.

Dick Miller stood between Piper and the phone and took off his belt.

"She ain't our youngen," Mrs. Miller warned her husband in a hushed voice.

"She may not be our youngen, but she's in our house," Dick Miller growled. "Only way to teach 'em right is with the belt. You know that."

Ring. Ring.

Piper burned with the need to answer the phone. If only she could fly—fly to the phone, fly to her mother, fly away from Dick Miller.

"It's high time you start following the rules same as everyone else," Dick breathed. "You ain't special, and for once you'll get treated like all the rest."

Ring. Ring.

Piper could stand it no longer. She threw herself forward, rushing past Mr. Miller and grabbing for the phone. In her haste her foot clumsily caught on Dick Miller's large boot, and she was sent sprawling. Her legs tangled up, and her right shoulder hit the floor with a thud. She landed in a heap at Dick Miller's feet. The phone, which she had only just managed to grab, was yanked free of her grasp as she fell.

Dick Miller looked down at Piper and restrung his worn cowhide belt. "Saved me the trouble of using this," he smirked.

The phone was dangling back and forth above Piper's head. She could hear the tinny voice of Betty McCloud from the receiver.

"Piper? Piper, are you there?"

Dick holstered the receiver into the cradle, disconnecting the call.

"If they don't come for her tonight, she sleeps in the cellar," he said. "Don't want the likes of her upstairs with the rest of us."

CHAPTER

20

THE CELLAR BENEATH THE MILLER house was stocked with shelves heavy with jams and preserves, pickled cucumbers and deviled eggs. Strung from the ceiling were large bunches of rosemary, thyme, bay leaves, and other herbs. Large sacks of flour, sugar, and wheat rested against the lower shelves, as well as tubs of molasses and honey. A cot had been wedged into the middle of all of this. Sally Sue had scrounged a single blanket and laid it on top of Piper to provide her with warmth. So arranged, Piper had been left in the darkness to endure the night.

Piper lay awake thinking about her new sister and what it had felt like to hold her. She was going to be a patient big sister, she decided. She was going to play with Jane and do things with her. She would tell her stories and make dolls with her, and they would always be close.

She guessed the time to be near dawn when she heard the lock on the cellar door being slowly and carefully pulled back. It was followed by the sound of halting footsteps creeping down the steps.

"Are you awake?" Jimmy Joe directed the beam of his flashlight into Piper's face.

Piper blinked, using her hand to shield her eyes. "Can you take that light out of my eye?"

Jimmy Joe dropped the beam to the floor and considered the cellar and Piper's place in it. "So . . . is it true? You really can't fly no more?"

Piper fixed Jimmy Joe with an "are you crazy" stare. "If I could fly, you think I'd be down here?"

Jimmy Joe perched on the top of the barrel of molasses, thinking on this. "Shoot. That's a kick in the head."

"You can say that again." Piper found it surprising that Jimmy Joe wasn't using her predicament as an opportunity to gloat, like his father had. Strangely, he looked genuinely sorry.

"Did you really do all those things you said?"

"What things?"

"You know, going over the Grand Canyon. Seeing that fish that looked like a monster?"

"Sure I did." Wincing from the pain in her shoulder, Piper attempted to sit up. "That and so much more. SO much more.

"There's a lot going on in the world, and we—my friends and me—we've been everywhere and seen it all. When you're up high looking down on things, it's so quiet. It gives you perspective, I guess. It's only when you're stuck down on the ground that everything gets so loud and hectic." It was too difficult to sit up, and so Piper contented herself with lying on her side. "One time, I was flying over this herd of elephants, and there was a baby elephant that got hurt. The mother elephant stopped to take care of it, but what she didn't see were the four lions in the long grass stalking them. When the lions saw the baby with the mama off by themselves, they attacked. I remember hovering in the air, and I was so scared for that baby, but there wasn't anything I could do. Well, the whole group of elephants came charging back to that mama and her baby, and they formed a circle around her. Then the biggest elephant started stomping its foot at the lions, squishing them. Didn't take long for those lions to take off and leave them be. I flew home with a smile on my face. It just goes to show you that we got to look out for each other. That's what I think. And I wouldn't have seen it if I hadn't been flying."

"Is that so?" Jimmy Joe shook his head in wonder. "I wish I could have seen that."

"There's a lot to see in this world. That's for sure."

Jimmy Joe reached into his pocket and brought out a

small piece of tightly folded paper. Carefully, he unfolded it bit by bit until it was all undone and he could smooth it out on his leg. He read it and then held it up for her to see. Even in the darkness, Piper recognized it.

"That's the sign I made for my flying lessons. How'd you get that?"

"I ripped it down," Jimmy Joe admitted.

"Oh. I guess I now know why no one came looking for flying lessons."

Jimmy Joe fingered it in a way that led Piper to believe that he'd spent a lot of time looking it over. "I've been thinking about it." Jimmy Joe got to his feet resolutely. "I want to fly and see and do all those things you did. I'm ready to start flying lessons."

"But I already told you I can't fly anymore."

Jimmy Joe shrugged his shoulders. "Those who can't do, teach."

Piper opened her mouth to point out other problems with this idea when faint noises from above caught Jimmy Joe's attention. His head snapped up, watching the floorboards, panic on his face. It wouldn't do for his father to find him in the cellar with Piper.

"Meet me in the pine grove after morning chores," he whispered, mounting the stairs gingerly to favor his hurt foot.

Piper sat up. "Jimmy Joe?"

Jimmy Joe paused, turning.

"When you hurt your foot, were you trying to fly?"

Jimmy Joe's face flushed. "None of your beeswax," he huffed, going up the stairs.

CHAPTER

21

*P*IPER WAITED AT THE CELLAR DOOR until Millie Mae saw fit to unlock it. Only then did she inform Piper that Betty had called not a moment before. She'd just missed her, in fact, which was a real shame, because if Piper had been handy, Millie Mae would have put her on the phone. According to Millie Mae, Betty said she had to stay another day in the hospital because the doctors didn't want to release her yet. Betty also wanted to make sure that Piper was staying put on the Miller farm.

"Which means I've got you on my hands for another day. The Lord gives us only what we can handle, but I declare he's testing me today."

"But the baby," Piper breathed. "Is the baby alright? And my ma?"

"We can only hope for the best." Millie Mae shook her head in a way that suggested she was expecting the worst. "A woman your mother's age has no business going around having babies. Phhhh." Millie Mae puffed air from her lungs. "Having babies can be a tricky business. I've seen new mothers look just fine, and then the next moment we're planning their funerals. There's just no telling with these things."

After those happy words, Millie Mae set about ordering Piper around and telling her in no small measure how poor her efforts were. Her mending was pathetic and her cleaning skills deplorable, and Millie Mae declared that a dirty windstorm did a better job of folding laundry. Even Sally Sue sent sympathetic looks Piper's way. It was a great relief to Piper to escape to the grove of pines after chores, where she found Jimmy Joe jumping off a large rock.

When she had first come up with the idea of starting a flying school, Piper hadn't actually gotten to the point of figuring out a lesson plan or any other practical ways she would get ordinary people to do extraordinary things. As she set about teaching Jimmy Joe to fly, she saw that it was no easy task.

"Stop jumping off things—you'll only get yourself banged up," Piper warned. "You've got to get real still and focus. Think about the sky."

Jimmy Joe attempted this for the better part of three seconds and then wanted to jump off something again.

They compromised on having him dangle from a tree branch that hung six feet off the ground. As he dangled, Jimmy Joe swung back and forth like a monkey.

"Close your eyes," Piper said. "Think about the sky. If you can think about it long enough, your body'll start to tingle, and then you'll get real light and floaty."

Jimmy Joe squinched his face up like the effort was causing him great pain. "How long 'fore the tingling starts?"

"Don't tense up like that. You gotta relax into it."

"Are you sure you know what you're doing?"

Piper was not sure at all. "Just keep at it."

Jimmy Joe hung from the branch, waiting for the tingling. Piper watched and waited along with him. Right off the bat, Piper could tell that Jimmy Joe was not going to be a natural. She was thinking about other ways to get him flying when suddenly a sharp wind whipped past her, blowing her hair about. When Piper pushed back her tousled locks, Myrtle was standing in front of her.

"Myrtle!" Piper jumped to her feet, electrified by the sight of her friend. "What's happening? Where is everyone? Are they back at the farm? Boy, do I have a lot to tell you."

Myrtle held up her hand to stop Piper's questions. "Piper, I've got to get back."

"But you *just* got here!"

Jimmy Joe's eyes snapped open, and the sight of Myrtle caused him to release his hold. He dropped out of the tree and fell to the ground with a thud, landing on his wounded toe. "Ouch!"

Myrtle registered Jimmy Joe's existence. "Who's that?"

"Jimmy Joe," Piper explained. Myrtle looked confused. "He's our closest neighbor, Myrtle. Don't you remember?" Piper sighed. "The Millers have the farm next to ours."

"Oh, right. The local." Myrtle did not use the word "local" in an affectionate way. More like she'd say "racist" or "ignoramus." "Why are you hanging out with him?"

"I'm trying to teach him to fly."

"Good luck with that," Myrtle said, then snorted and turned her back on him entirely. "Conrad sent me."

"Where is he? What's happening?"

"We got to Xanthia, and the first thing Conrad did was request an audience with Elder Equilla."

"Elder Equilla agreed to meet?" Piper was amazed. Elder Equilla was over 150 years old and, as the oldest Chosen One, was the head of the council of elders. She rarely granted audiences, and especially not to Outsiders.

"Elder Equilla made them wait, but Conrad insisted.

When Elder Equilla finally met with us, Conrad explained to her about the bugs. He told her that without the help of the Chosen Ones, all Outsiders would be thrown into chaos."

Jimmy Joe hobbled over, listening closely.

"And?" Piper prompted.

"He pleaded for their help, but it's not looking good," Myrtle said. "Elder Equilla said that nothing could be done until the council of elders deliberated on it. They have promised to give us a decision by sundown, but we've learned that they are building a wall right now."

"What kind of wall?"

"They're sealing off Xanthia so that no one can ever leave it again. Or enter it, either. Conrad thinks that Elder Equilla is stalling until the wall is done. If you ask me, it's hopeless."

Unlike Myrtle, Piper had optimism. But she had also spent enough time in Xanthia to make a friend there: AnnA. AnnA had explained to Piper how the Chosen Ones were a peace-loving people of surpassing gentleness. They abhorred Outsiders, which is what they called anyone who didn't live in Xanthia, precisely because they considered them violent. AnnA was so kind, though, and Piper knew the Chosen Ones were just like her.

"The Chosen Ones are good people," Piper pointed

out. "Now that Conrad has explained everything to them and they know how much we need their help, they'll come to our aid. I know it."

Myrtle looked at Piper skeptically, but then again, Myrtle had been born into extreme poverty and had known hunger. In her early years she had seen many things, some of them violent. It wasn't that Piper hadn't had her share of troubles, but somehow she had maintained a sunny disposition, which was something Myrtle had never had. The first time Piper flew, it was for the joy of it; the first time Myrtle ran, it was to escape danger and harm; that distinction made all the difference in their dispositions.

"What can I do to help?" Piper leaned in eagerly.

"You can't do anything. Listen, Piper, I have to get back, but Conrad sent me to warn you. He said . . ." Myrtle put her hand on her throat and cleared it. "'Piper, my experiment came back, and the venom is still working on you at a cellular level. It's still changing you, reprogramming your DNA.'"

"What does that mean?"

Myrtle held up a finger. "'I know you're going to wonder what that means. It means you could be in danger. It means that if the bugs aren't stopped and they blast, it could set off something inside of you. You must take great care.'"

Piper's mouth formed an O.

Jimmy Joe looked from Piper to Myrtle. "Uh. What in the heck are you two talking about?"

"That if the bugs blast, they could blow Piper up, idiot," Myrtle said, not bothering to look at Jimmy Joe.

"Hey, don't call me an idiot!"

"Then stop eavesdropping on conversations that don't concern you." Myrtle crossed her arms over her chest and once again placed her back to Jimmy Joe. "Conrad didn't want to alarm you, but until he comes back, he wanted you to be . . . careful."

Piper expelled the air in her lungs slowly, suddenly very aware of every movement she made. "Careful how?"

"Just careful." Myrtle looked at her watch. "I've got to go."

"Let me go with you. Please! I want to help." Piper grabbed Myrtle's hand. "I don't belong here, Myrtle. I don't fit in."

Myrtle gently pried Piper's hand away. "You can't come with us, Piper. Conrad says you need to get used to the way you are now. " She turned to go. "Oh yes, I almost forgot. Do you remember that girl AnnA?"

"Yes!" Piper brightened up at the thought of gentle, shy AnnA.

"She says Asanti." Myrtle bowed as she said the word.

This was a typical greeting of the Chosen Ones, and out of habit, Piper returned the bow. "She wanted me to let you know that she blossomed."

"That's great news!"

"What's blossoming?" Jimmy Joe's brow screwed up over the word.

"In Xanthia, when a Chosen One's extraordinary ability is revealed, it is called blossoming," Piper explained. "AnnA was a late bloomer, and she was worried she might not have a gift."

"Oh." Jimmy Joe chewed on that information for a moment before asking, "So? What's her gift?"

Piper turned to Myrtle expectantly. "Yeah, what's her gift?"

"She's a jumper." Myrtle's eyebrow shot up significantly. "Gotta go." With that, she threw off a salute and left nothing but a gust of wind that picked up dry and dirty leaves and scattered them in Jimmy Joe's face.

Jimmy Joe coughed and waved them away. It seemed more than a coincidence at this point that whenever Myrtle came and went, he was the only recipient of her dirty exhaust.

"What in the heck was that all about? What's a jumper?" Jimmy Joe said through a cough.

"Beats me! Maybe she can jump really high, like a grasshopper."

"Why would anyone want to do that?"

"It's not like we get to decide our ability," Piper pointed out. "It just happens."

Jimmy Joe dug his toe into the dirt. "So then I can't decide to be a flier? No matter how hard I try?"

Seeing the knit of concern on Jimmy Joe's brow, Piper thought about it. "I don't know. My ma says I just started floating when I was a tiny baby. Of course I remember deciding I wanted to turn my floating into flying, but I don't actually remember how I came to float."

"Huh." Jimmy Joe started back to the farm, and Piper joined him. They walked in silence, side by side. When the barn came into view, Piper stopped.

"How come you want to fly all of a sudden?"

"Dunno." Jimmy Joe rubbed the back of his hand against his nose and sniffed loudly. "I just wanna be good at something. Rory Ray and my bothers are always picking on me, putting me down. I'm sick of it. If I could fly, then I'd show 'em, and they'd have to give me respect. Are you sure there isn't something I can do to fly? How'd you do it?"

"I wish I knew." Piper sighed, letting out a long stream of air through her nostrils. "Before, it felt easier than falling off a log. Now I can't wrap my mind around how I ever got up there." Piper's hand went to her shoulder, where she'd fallen on it the night before. She moved it around painfully, stretching out the muscle. "But I also used to feel different, too. I felt like I was . . . buoyant. Like I was filled up with hope and life."

"You don't feel like that now?"

"Not so much. Not like I did before." Piper winced and held the place on her shoulder that hurt.

"I can get you help for that." Jimmy Joe flicked his head in the direction of her shoulder.

"What kind of help?"

"Meet me in the hayloft in an hour." Jimmy Joe took off running at full tilt and left Piper in the field to make her own way back.

CHAPTER

22

*T*HE MILLER BARN, FROM THE OUTSIDE, was almost exactly the same as the McClouds'. Unlike the McCloud barn, it was filled with hay, feed, and animals. After an hour had passed, Piper cautiously approached the loft door, careful not to draw attention to herself. No sooner had she wrapped her hand around the latch than Jimmy Joe pulled her inside.

"Pa's at the pigpen at the back of the barn, so keep quiet," he warned. "C'mon over here."

Jimmy Joe led Piper past banks of hay bales until they arrived at a table next to which stood Rory Ray Miller in a marine uniform. On the table was a medical kit that was about the size of shoebox covered in a green camouflage pattern, tightly packed with an array of battlefield necessities.

"Take a seat, soldier," Rory Ray ordered, pointing

to a bale in front of him. Piper sat down, and Rory Ray nodded to Jimmy Joe. "Get lost, pest."

"I wanna stay," Jimmy Joe whined.

Rory Ray kicked at him, hitting his butt. "When I need a whiny crybaby, I'll come looking for you. Till then, beat it."

Rory Ray was about twice Jimmy Joe's size, and Jimmy Joe didn't want Piper to see him get beat up, so he took off with what little dignity he could muster. He hated it when his brothers treated him like that. One day he was gonna show them.

"Where'd you get hit?" Rory Ray demanded of Piper.

"I fell down. You know that."

"I asked you a question, soldier!" Rory Ray barked.

Piper pointed to her shoulder, and Rory Ray pulled out some surgical gloves and snapped them on. When they were in place, he lifted her arm with surprising gentleness and moved it about.

"Don't think it's broken, but you've got some bruising. I'll bind it up to relieve any strain and get you back to active duty." Rory Ray took out a bandage and began to wind it over Piper's arm and shoulder.

"I ordered this online," Rory Ray explained when Piper wondered at the kit. "Every good soldier needs to be trained in basic trauma care to help themselves or a fellow soldier if they require medical assistance while in the line of duty."

It sounded to Piper like Rory Ray was reciting something he'd read. She tried to stay still while he worked on her and watched as Rory Ray bit his lip and bunched his eyebrows together, focusing all his attention.

"I didn't know that you wanted to be a soldier, Rory Ray."

"I'm going to be a marine," he corrected. "And why wouldn't I want to be a marine? We live in a great country. It needs to be defended and protected, and it's up to the armed forces to do that. It's a privilege to serve." Rory Ray shook his head as though explaining such a thing to someone like Piper was useless. "You wouldn't understand."

"Why wouldn't I understand?"

"You and your type don't care about things like that." Rory Ray wound the bandage over Piper's arm and crossed it over her chest snuggly.

Piper was affronted. "All we do is try to stop threats to this country and other countries too."

Rory Ray snorted, disbelieving. "Yeah, right."

"Just what do you think we're doing all the time?"

"I see you flying off places, acting all important. And those friends of yours, putting their noses up in the air, like they're so special. Probably going off to parties."

Piper was aghast. "We never put our noses up in the air. And we never once went to a party, and I wasn't acting important when I was flying: I was busy. Max is out there right now probably blowing up some building or poisoning some water source or heaven knows what, and I can't even help with it."

Rory Ray looked skeptical.

"That's the truth, Rory Ray. And, by the way, you know that drought we had last year that was killing all the crops? If it hadn't been for Ahmed and Nalen bringing in some rain, your fields would have withered and died."

This information caught Rory Ray's attention. "No way."

"Yes way," Piper insisted. "They're weather changers. Whipping up a rainstorm doesn't even cause them to break a sweat. They've got enough power in their fingertips to start hurricanes and enough precision to train a gentle wind to move a cloud at no more than one mile an hour."

"You're making that up."

"I am not making it up." Piper suddenly winced. "Ouch."

"Hold still."

Piper paused to let the pain settle. "All I'm saying is that we want the same thing. And you can believe that or not, but it's the truth."

Rory Ray completed his work and carefully packed away his materials into the case. "Ma always said that you aren't right in the head."

Piper sighed. Getting to her feet, she turned to him. "And do you believe that?"

"Ma says—"

"I know what your ma says, but what do *you* think?"

No one had ever asked Rory Ray what he thought. It was a strict policy of Dick Miller's that if there was thinking to be done around the Miller place, he'd be the one doing it. What did he think? For the first time, Rory Ray attempted to venture into parts of his brain that had never been touched. It made his head feel itchy.

"If you're going to be a marine, you'd better be able to think straight and clear," Piper said. As she walked away, she realized that the bandage had relieved all the pain in her shoulder, and she was grateful for the help. "It feels better," she said, stopping. "Thanks, Rory Ray, you did a good job."

"It's what marines do," he said, and shrugged.

*T*HAT NIGHT, AS PIPER LAY ON HER COT in the darkness of the cellar, she could hear Mr. and Mrs. Miller talking above her.

"I want her out of this house," Dick said, not bothering to lower his voice. "If I have to see her face at the table for one more meal, I'll throw something."

"Oh, Dick, no."

Stomping feet made the floorboards quake above Piper's head and sent dust showering down over her.

"Betty and Joe McCloud probably don't want to come back and get her. I wouldn't be surprised if they're trying to figure a way to dump her off on us."

"You can't think that!"

"Can't I? Betty's got her hands on a nice new baby with nothing wrong with it, and she won't want that youngen anywhere near it. I wouldn't."

"Shhhh, Dick, you shouldn't say such things."

"I'll talk as I see fit, Millie Mae. Mark my words: they won't be back to pick her up anytime soon."

"Now, Dick—"

Stomp. Stomp.

"Dick, don't get yourself into a state!"

Slam! went the front door.

"Dick, come back!"

Dick didn't come back, and eventually, Millie Mae's soft tread padded across the floor and mounted the stairs, and the house was quiet.

The cellar was blackness, and Piper lay still. Above her, Dick Miller's words wormed their way through the floorboards, wafting down and burrowing into her skin. Piper curled into a ball beneath the thin blanket, shielding as much of her body as she could. She felt a burning in her stomach and back. It wasn't physically painful, but it was uncomfortable; it felt like a brewing storm of sadness, doubt, and confusion. Suddenly, a red glow filled the room, and, looking down at herself, Piper saw that the light was coming from her—from inside her. She was glowing just like one of the bugs.

Taking the blanket, Piper wrapped it tightly around her middle, blocking out the glow in the only way she could think of. Conrad's warning blazed in her mind, and she took great care not to move. It took several hours more for her to find sleep.

CHAPTER

24

*T*HERE WASN'T A SOUND AT THE MILLER table except for the ringing of the phone.

Ring. Ring.

Piper kept her eyes on her plate and didn't move a muscle, didn't breathe. Even so, Dick Miller was on the verge of blowing, every ring of the telephone notching his anger and frustration to new heights. His hands, curled into fists around his fork and knife, were planted on the table. He glared over his roast beef at Piper, willing her to give him a reason to lash out.

Ring. Ring.

Piper silently prayed for the phone to stop. After the day she'd had, this was the cherry on top. Dick Miller had sent her out to the south field to pick rocks all morning. After every spring plow, new rocks came to the surface and had to be hand picked and thrown off to the side of the field. This was a thankless task, more punishment than anything, and Dick Miller felt it was just the thing for Piper to do. After that, Millie Mae had handed her a basket of clothes that needed mending. While Piper was bent over an old pair of Dick Miller's underpants, attempting to darn a large hole in the rear end, Millie Mae told her in no uncertain terms she was completely useless with a needle and showed no hope of ever improving.

"You can't do nothing," Millie Mae sniffed. "You can't cook or mend or knit or fold. I don't know what you've been doing with yourself all these years, but it sure hasn't amounted to anything."

As this sentiment was settling over Piper, it was time for supper. No sooner had the table been set and the blessing said than the phone started.

Ring. Ring.

Betty had called first thing that morning to say that she wasn't expecting to be released from the hospital. Was this ringing phone bringing more news? How was the baby?

Despite Piper's yearning to talk to her mother, it no longer occurred to her to reach for the phone, and it was a mercy when at last the phone gave up and stopped ringing.

Dick smacked his lips, gaining satisfaction that at the very least Piper had been thwarted. "A man can't eat his meal in peace with all this," he said, nodding at the phone. "I won't have it."

"I made your favorite for you," Millie Mae said, fussing. "Get some of that in your stomach and it'll make you feel better."

Dick roughly tore some meat off with his fork, jamming it into a pool of gravy. He lifted it to his open mouth, ready to enjoy his meal—

BANG! BANG! A fist hammered on the front door.

The unexpected thrashing sent every single person at the Miller table onto their feet.

Dick Miller threw down his uneaten food. The fork landed in the gravy, which splattered in all directions. He pounded his fist upon the table. "Sit down!" he barked.

Everyone sat.

"We DO NOT answer the door during dinner!" he roared at Piper as though somehow she were responsible. "That door stays shut."

The front door swung open.

Standing in the threshold was none other than Stark Raven, the sight of whom made Dick Miller take a step back and Millie Mae gasp.

"I knocked as loud as I could," Stark Raven said, sweeping into the room uninvited. She was wearing a bright yellow top with baggy purple pants, over which she had thrown a thick woven cape of every shade of green. In her hand was a walking stick, worn smooth from use, and on her shoulder perched a blue budgie that hopped about excitedly.

"How do, Millie Mae?" Stark Raven nodded. Nervously Millie Mae returned the greeting with a faint wave of her fingers. "You haven't come calling to my door in a long time."

"Oh, no, I haven't," Millie Mae muttered.

"I've been looking for you!" Stark Raven said, pointing the stick at Piper.

Piper cast a nervous glance in Dick Miller's direction to see if there was any danger that he might be taking off his belt. The redness was draining from Dick Miller's face, and his beady eyes cast back and forth as though looking to escape his face.

"We're eating dinner," Dick said, but his voice had lost conviction. "We're not having visitors right now."

"Well, I didn't come to see you, did I?" Stark Raven said. "I'm here to talk to Piper McCloud."

Piper bit her lip to stop her face from turning into a smile. Dick Miller rocked from side to side like a top.

"She can't talk right now," he said. "This is my house and my rules. You'll have to come back."

"Well, I'm not coming back," Stark Raven stated flatly. "I've got important business with Piper, and it's up to her whether she wants to talk to me or not. It's no business of yours."

Dick Miller raised a finger in the air to make a point, but Stark Raven ignored him and turned to Piper. "Piper, I've got some news that I think you'll be wanting to hear. Let's talk on the porch away from"—Stark Raven waved her hand dismissively at Dick Miller— "any distractions."

Piper sprang to her feet and followed Stark Raven out of the house and onto the porch, keenly aware that the Millers had abandoned the table altogether and gathered around the windows overlooking the porch to spy on them.

Stark Raven was filled with an excitement that fueled a pacing back and forth. "You should sit yourself down," she instructed Piper, pointing her stick at the porch swing. Piper sat as instructed, albeit perching on the edge of the swing in a state of acute curiosity.

The sun was setting, and the fireflies were blinking across the lawn behind Stark Raven, creating a flickering halo around her. Now more than ever, she appeared part witch, part mythical creature.

"I heard something," she said, waving her stick as she spoke. "It's not important how I heard, but the rocks can speak if you find the right one. It took me a while." She waved the stick again as though dismissing the whole thing altogether. "This is what they had to say. Turns out them bugs are thousands of years old and used to be as common as houseflies. Quiet peaceful creatures that nested in forests and didn't bother no one. Then one day this boy came along, and he tricked them."

"A boy?" Piper jumped to her feet. "I bet it was Max. That sounds like something he'd do."

Stark Raven waved her down so that she could continue. "The bugs got a shell, and they get to a certain age and they've got to shed it, like a skin, and then they become something else. I don't know what. Max jumbled up their thoughts so that they forgot how to shed their shell. Then they all got stuck inside themselves and caught up and couldn't get out. They grew big, but the shell kept them small, and this drove them mad."

Stark Raven got a look in her eyes like *she* was going mad, or at least understood the madness. "That's when people found a way to put the bugs to sleep, for their own protection."

"I saw a cave drawing," Piper said. "The bugs started attacking people."

"That's what happens when you don't feel comfortable in your own body—the pain starts bursting out and going all over the place." Suddenly Stark Raven sat on the railing, exhausted. The blue budgie on her shoulder, which had been hopping about during her explanation, now nuzzled her earlobe comfortingly.

"It would be just like Max to cause trouble like that." Piper could picture the whole thing in her mind's eye. Max was always on the lookout for mischief. "He loves to cause problems and then feed off the energy so that he'll stay young."

"Hmmm." Stark shook her head in bursts. "It's a terrible state. Terrible. Those bugs will die if they don't shed their shells."

Piper thought about the blasting that they did and wondered how that was related to the shedding. Was it possible that they were trying to blast their shells off?

Stark Raven got to her feet, shaking herself slightly. "Well, I've got to be going."

"Already?" Piper followed behind her. "But wait—I want to help. What am I supposed to do?"

"Dunno." Stark Raven trudged down the steps and started across the yard. Piper stayed close on her heels.

"Did you find out anything else? Is there a way to help the bugs shed?"

"Dunno."

"But how come I can't fly?" Piper tugged on Stark Raven's shawl. "And Conrad says I might be in danger. He says I've got bug venom in me and it could blow. What should I do?"

"How should I know?"

"But Millie Mae says there's no point to me and I'm a waste of time."

Stark Raven stopped in her tracks. "Now why would you listen to a word that comes out of Millie Mae Miller's mouth?"

Piper bit her lip. "But I'm normal like they are now. Wouldn't she know?"

Stark Raven snorted. "You ain't normal. You're never gonna be normal. There's no such thing as normal. We come into this world, and each one of us is as different as snowflakes, none of us like the one that came before. Some folks trick themselves into thinking they're the same, but they ain't. It's up to you to decide who you are and what makes you special, and no one's gonna help you do that, least of all Millie Mae Miller."

Piper remained frozen, letting Stark Raven's words settle into her insides.

Stark Raven patted Piper on the arm. "The only answers you'll ever find are inside yourself. No one gets to decide what you're worth—only you. That's what I say."

⚬ ⚬

DICK MILLER PRESSED HIS FACE TO THE window and watched as Stark Raven merged back into the forest, leaving Piper alone in the yard. Now that Piper was no longer with Stark Raven, his anger returned with greater force so that by the time she turned back to the house, he was a kettle at full boil.

Piper quietly opened the front door and stepped inside, and this was all it took to make Dick Miller explode.

"I want you out of this house right now!" he yelled. "GET OUT!"

Piper considered Dick Miller's lobster face and his red, throbbing finger pointing outward.

"You don't belong around decent people. OUT! Get out!" Dick waved his finger some more.

"I wanted to get to know y'all," Piper said quietly. "I thought maybe I could be like you. I may not have done a good job, but I did try my hardest." Piper looked to Rory Ray and Jimmy Joe. "We're neighbors. It's crazy that we don't know each other better and think all these things about each other that aren't even true."

"I know what's true and what's not," Dick Miller roared, jabbing his finger in the air at Piper like a sword. "Don't try to fool me."

Piper flinched. "I'm just saying that maybe we could be more friendly to each other."

"Friendly? We don't need friends like you. It'll be a cold day when we come calling at your door."

With each insult Dick Miller hurled at Piper, she curled in on herself, holding more tightly to her stomach.

Dick Miller reached for his belt and unlatched it. "I'll do what I should have done when you walked through this door; I'll teach you a lesson, girl."

Millie Mae gasped, pointing at Piper. "Heavens to Betsy!" A red glow was pulsing out of Piper's stomach.

Piper groaned, holding herself as the light grew brighter.

"Pa," Jimmy Joe said quietly, his voice shaking. "She's supposed to be careful. Those others said she could blow up."

"Pffff. Was I talking to you, boy?" Dick Miller turned on Jimmy Joe. Jimmy Joe prepared for the belt to come his way, but before Dick Miller could swing it, Rory Ray stepped between them, his eyes blazing.

"What's this? You got something to say, boy?" Dick Miller roared at Rory Ray. "You think you got the brains to open your mouth and say something?"

Rory Ray fumbled, willing but unable to speak.

"Ohhhh." Piper grabbed on to the door frame to support herself. The light inside her was so red and bright now it hurt the Millers to look at her. "I'm going home now. I don't want to stay here anymore."

"You'll do as I say."

"No," Piper said quietly with command. "I'll do as I say. I don't belong here."

With that, Piper walked out the door, not bothering to close it behind her.

Dick Miller's body stiffened like he'd been jolted by a strong current of electricity. He didn't like being spoken to in such a fashion. He didn't like it. Particularly because what Piper said rang clearly of truth, and the truth burns in deeper places.

"You never come back here. You aren't welcome. You bring nothing but trouble wherever you go. You hear me?"

Piper could hear him loud and clear, but still she did not listen. Holding on to her throbbing, glowing body, she began to walk home.

CHAPTER

25

*T*HE DARK OF NIGHT WAS BLEEDING OUT the blue of day in the sky above her as Piper stumbled down the road toward home. She had purposely avoided looking at the sky for days, but the calm that came over her at the thought of her release from the Miller household gave her hope, and that made her look up. It was such a sky—she filled her lungs with it. She'd flown on countless such nights but had never once thought during those flights that her time in the sky might be fleeting. She wished that she had savored it more.

How exactly had she done it? The actual mechanics of flying slipped further and further away, like water running through her fingers. What had it felt like to glide through the air?

Conrad had said the bugs were circling the globe right now. According to Stark Raven's news, they were also longing for their own release from the cramped enclosure of their shell. She couldn't see them, but she imagined where they might be.

Piper inhaled deeply and then again. The night air was a balm to the burning in her stomach, and the red glow dimmed and then flickered like a candle in a strong breeze.

"Piper! Piper!"

Piper turned to see Jimmy Joe running toward her, dusk closing in around him. "Ma says you're to come back," Jimmy Joe called out. "She says she gave her word to your ma and means to look after you until she gets back."

"I'm not going with you." Piper picked up her pace again. "I tried my hardest. I'm never going to fit in at your house, and I don't even want to try anymore. Tell your ma that I've made up my mind and I'm going home."

Jimmy Joe came up next to her, matching her pace and panting from his run. "But she said I had to get you."

"I'm not going, Jimmy Joe."

Jimmy Joe loped next to Piper, not sure how this was to be resolved. He wasn't prepared to physically drag Piper back to his farm, and if she wouldn't come willingly, that didn't leave him many choices. "So what are you gonna do now?"

"Go home."

Jimmy Joe looked over his shoulder. "My ma's gonna be sore when you're not with me."

"Just remind her how *different* I am."

Jimmy Joe laughed and Piper joined him. "You sure you're okay?" Jimmy Joe nodded to the strange red glow in her stomach area.

"It's been calming itself down. Last time this happened it took a while, but then it went away." Piper shrugged it off. "That'll probably happen this time too."

"Okay." Jimmy Joe stopped. "Well, I guess this is good-bye."

Seeing that he meant to leave, Piper stopped too.

Jimmy Joe held out his hand. Piper took it and they shook.

"Maybe I'll see you around?"

"I'm sorry I didn't teach you how to fly."

"That's okay. I probably wouldn't have been any good at it anyway."

"I don't think that's true, Jimmy Joe. I think you'd have made a good flier. See you around."

Piper turned to go, and Jimmy Joe did the same, taking one last look over his shoulder at her. Piper hadn't been what he'd thought at all. He'd seen no traces of the wickedness his ma had warned him about. He was considering this when suddenly he felt the ground shake and turn to a jumble beneath his feet. Because this made absolutely no sense to him, he stopped and looked down in confusion. By the time he realized that running away would have been a better choice, it was too late, and he was already knee-deep and stuck.

"Ahhh!"

The timbre of Jimmy Joe's scream told Piper there was trouble, and when she saw him sinking, his face the picture of shocked horror as the ground bubbled and quaked around him, she started. Jimmy Joe had no idea what was happening to him. Piper, on the other hand, knew exactly what was going on.

"Don't move!" Piper ran to Jimmy Joe. He was sinking quickly. Throwing herself down, Piper crawled as close as she could to the hole.

"Grab my hand," she said, reaching out to him.

Jimmy Joe latched on to her. Right next to him, a long black insect leg came thrusting out of the dirt, the sight of which made Jimmy Joe scream again.

With all her might, Piper pulled, but Jimmy Joe was heavy, and she didn't have the strength to pull him out.

"Don't let me go!" Jimmy Joe was falling fast.

Piper's grip was loosening. Jimmy Joe's fingers were slowly slipping out of her grasp. "Hold on!"

Suddenly, another set of arms reached over Piper and latched hold of Jimmy Joe. With a mighty tug, those arms popped him up and over the side to safety.

"Get moving!" Rory Ray screamed. He was in his full marine uniform with a knapsack over his shoulder, apparently ready to do battle. In the next moment, he was dragging Piper and Jimmy Joe away from the forming crater. They took cover behind a large rock, peeking over it at the black bug.

The bug thrashed about, flapping its wings and shaking off the dirt.

"Cover your ears," Piper warned the two boys.

Sure enough, the bug let out an ear-shattering screech.

Rory Ray's eyes were moons, so wide that Piper could see in them the reflection of the bug stretching out its wings. After several attempts, the bug lifted off and started into the sky. Inside her core, Piper felt an overpowering need to ascend—to burst out, to go up. Abandoning her hiding spot, she stood out in the open, watching the bug go up, up to the stars.

Now that the bug was gone, the drama and excitement dissipated quickly, the quiet of the night returned, and the three of them were left next to a large hole on a country road. Piper breathed out her yearning.

"Well, there goes another one," she said.

Rory Ray's mouth opened. "It was just like you

said," he wheezed. "There are giant bugs coming out of the ground."

"I told you so. Don't know why you think I'm a liar when I never once told a lie to you."

Jimmy Joe was shaking so much his legs buckled.

"You're okay, Jimmy Joe." Piper dusted him off. "It didn't bite you. It's when you get bit that you've got bigger problems."

Gathering herself, Piper headed toward home. "If you come across another one, just get out of its way and you'll be fine."

"Wait!" Rory Ray croaked, his voice hoarse and dry. "Wait!"

CHAPTER

26

*P*IPER WAS MOST OF THE WAY UP HER driveway before the shell-shocked Rory Ray, and later Jimmy Joe, were able to catch up to her. Joe McCloud had arranged for Milton Mooney to take care of the animals while he was at the hospital, but Milton had finished up hours before so that the farm was quiet and settled for the night.

"Wait!" Rory Ray's legs were unsteady next to Piper's sure gait. "What—that, that thing—what was that?"

"It's a bug. Like I said." Piper shrugged. "According to what I've seen, the bugs give off a blast. It's like an electromagnetic burst, but we'd need Conrad to explain it scientifically. The point is that if they all blast together, they'll burn out every computer, satellite, and communication system on the planet. It'll shut everything down and throw us back into the Dark Ages."

Rory Ray's head hurt again. "And that's something you guys, you and all your weird friends, can stop?"

"Yes and no. Yes, we want to, but this one's too big even for us, and Conrad and the others are off trying to get help from the Chosen Ones. Oh, you don't know about them, either. They live on Mother Mountain, that's in Xanthia, but no one has ever been there. They don't like Outsiders. It's a long story." Piper threw up her hands. She could hear herself and knew how it all sounded, knew that kids like the Millers would think it was crazy talk. "I don't know why I'm explaining this to you anyway, because you won't believe me. I might as well save my breath."

Rory Ray eyed Piper carefully. "You sure this isn't another one of your whoppers?"

Back to that? "Just forget it, Rory Ray. Go home. I've got things to do."

Wrapping her hand around the handle of the old barn door, Piper waited for it to complete her identity scan. The barn door opened, and she stepped inside, activating the light sensors as well as the monitors. Piper headed for the team-meeting table, where the 3-D computer projected the globe that showed the current positions of all the bugs.

Following Piper into the barn, first Rory Ray and, soon after, Jimmy Joe, stopped dead in their tracks as the sheer impossibility of the McCloud barn was displayed before them; the strange technology, things they had never seen or dreamed of, surrounded them at every turn.

Rory Ray pointed and looked, then turned and pointed more. Jimmy Joe stood still, his mouth open wide. Having just barely recovered from the sight of a giant bug thrusting itself out of the earth, their brains once again tried to rearrange around this new information.

Meanwhile, Piper sat up on the meeting table and reached for the globe, turning it and studying the positions of the bugs. Like a net surrounding the entire planet, their formation was almost complete.

"We don't have much time," Piper said to herself. "Computer, show me the current location of Conrad."

The globe flickered and then zoomed in on a mountainous region in the northwest. A flickering red dot throbbed like a heartbeat, indicating his position.

"Darn it—he's still in Xanthia." Piper wished she could reach him. The Chosen Ones abhorred technology, making it impossible to get a message in or out of the remote region unless you physically went there. What was taking him so long? If the bugs were ready to blast, the team should be on their way back already. Myrtle had told her the day before that Elder

Equilla was giving her decision at sunset. What were they doing?

"What the—!" Rory Ray screamed and hit the deck. Piper looked up in time to see Fido flap past the place Rory Ray's head had been moments before. He flew in his usual batty way so that he ended up crashing into Piper and, if she hadn't grabbed hold of him, would have flown right on by.

"Grarrrrr." Fido's long purple tongue unfurled to lick Piper.

"Calm down, Fido. You could have hurt yourself, flying like that." Piper pet Fido and then placed him back on the ground, where he circled excitedly around her feet. "I missed you, too."

Rory Ray cautiously got back up. "What in the heck is that?"

"That's Fido, Conrad's pet."

Fido flapped and scuttled over to greet the boys.

Rory Ray and Jimmy Joe looked at Fido's wings and his strange leathery skin that was more reptile than dog. When his purple tongue came darting out again, they braced themselves.

"I have never seen anything so ugly in my life." Jimmy Joe held his hands up to his chest so that he wouldn't accidentally touch Fido's strangeness.

"Is he . . . is he . . ." Once again, Rory Ray was on the verge of losing his voice. He also didn't seem to be quite able to form an appropriate question to encapsulate the strangeness that was Fido. "Is he . . . poisonous?"

Piper had to admit it was a fair question. "Could be." Fido wasn't the sort of pet that would ever bite anyone, though. "I think he likes you, Rory Ray. Give him a pat."

"You mean . . . touch him?" Rory Ray would have stuck his hand in fire before he willingly touched such a strange creature. "Maybe later." Or never.

Jimmy Joe started poking around the place, picking things up and turning them over. "What's this for?"

"Don't touch that. It's Conrad's time machine!"

"What's going on up in the loft?"

"What's that smell?"

"How'd you get the picture to float above the table like that?"

"In this here picture you all are by a pyramid. Is that fake?"

The boys' curiosity was endless, and they battered Piper with questions. Piper was happy to answer each one and even felt a growing sense of pride. This was her home; these were her things; she was in all the pictures with her friends.

And just as she was feeling better than she had in the longest time, Rory Ray had to go and say, "It's too bad you can't fly anymore and your friends left you behind the way they did."

Piper stopped short, the excitement and energy of being back seeped down her legs and welled by her ankles. "They'll be back. I can still help out."

Rory Ray raised his eyebrows. Under his breath he mumbled, "You help them? I'd like to see that."

Suddenly a loud clunk on the metal roof of the barn far above them made them all duck and crouch. The sound was so loud and unexpected they looked to each other for clues as to what was going on.

"What was that?"

Piper could hear scratching. Something or someone was on top of the barn. Standing back up, Piper cupped her hands over her mouth and called up.

"Hello! Who's up there?"

The noise disappeared, but moments later the chickens in the henhouse exploded in squawking and clucking sounds.

Jimmy Joe was at Piper's side by this point. "Sounds like you got a fox in your henhouse."

Piper ran out of the barn, Jimmy Joe right with her. They could both hear something big inside the henhouse knocking into the wood. Throwing open the door, Piper exposed it to be empty of everything but extremely agitated hens.

"Over here!" shouted Rory Ray.

Tearing out of the henhouse, they found Rory Ray wading through a hayrick next to the barn. Like the marine he wanted to be, he was charging full tilt at some large creature under the hay that was fitfully moaning and violently thrashing around.

"I've got it! I've got it!" Rory Ray dove on top of the creature, tackling it.

The creature let out a garbled cry.

"Make one more move and you're dead!" Rory Ray screamed.

Piper found Rory Ray's rhetoric harsh and made a mental note to speak with him about it when he wasn't in the middle of doing whatever it was he was doing.

Wrapping his arms around his quarry, Rory Ray lifted it up, dragging it out of the hayrick. When he was in the middle of the yard, he tossed the creature to the ground, preparing to subdue it further or prevent it from escaping or whatever else it might attempt.

Piper and Jimmy Joe gathered, forming a circle, also preparing themselves for any eventuality. They watched as a strange tangle of white cloth struggled about. There was something about the material that was familiar to Piper. As she leaned down, the odd creature untangled all at once, revealing that it wasn't a creature at all but a girl.

She was Piper's age, with long, auburn hair, an unblemished complexion, and absolute terror in her eyes. Piper recognized her instantly.

"AnnA!"

AnnA screamed!

"AnnA, it's okay. It's me . . . Piper."

AnnA was crouching, preparing for an assault. Piper reached out to steady her. "Don't be afraid. Nothing is going to hurt you."

"Someone said that I am to die!" AnnA trembled.

"That was Rory Ray, and he was being dramatic. No one is going to kill anyone." Except for Piper, who now had plans to kill Rory Ray. "This is Rory Ray, and this is Jimmy Joe. They're my neighbors. That means they live over there."

AnnA's eyes were wild and roving. Piper put her hands on either side of AnnA's face and forced AnnA to look at her and only her. "Look at me, AnnA. Look! It's Piper."

AnnA's chest panted up and down several times. "Piper?"

"Your friend. I'm your friend Piper. You're okay."

"You are Piper?" AnnA whispered.

"Yes! Your friend."

AnnA threw her arms around Piper and hugged her. Piper hugged AnnA back.

"Asanti," AnnA said.

"Asanti," Piper echoed.

"There is much to tell you," AnnA said, remembering her purpose and breaking free from the hug. "We must speak."

CHAPTER

27

ANNA WAS WEARING A DELICATE CLOTH that was wound about her and fastened in place around her waist. She was just as Piper remembered: a fragile, shy creature who wanted nothing more than to slide away and melt into the shadows. Piper settled her upon the porch steps, and Jimmy Joe fetched a glass of water for her.

AnnA wondered at the glass and at the way the barn was built and the way the land was flat and how there wasn't a place where they could fall into the valley as it was on Mother Mountain. The only thing that was not strange to AnnA was Fido.

"I have blossomed." AnnA was shy but happy to share the good news with Piper.

"Myrtle told me that you can jump," Piper said. "What does that mean?"

"I jump." AnnA moved her hand from one point to the next.

"You mean like a frog? Or a rabbit?"

The references confused AnnA. There were no frogs or rabbits in Xanthia.

"Do you jump up? Like high?" Piper started to demonstrate by jumping up and down.

Jimmy Joe jumped up and down too. "Do you jump like this?"

AnnA shook her head. "No. No, it is not that. I jump." Once again she moved her hand from here to there.

"I don't understand," said Piper. "Can you show me?"

Haltingly, AnnA got up off the bench and took several steps away. Claiming a part of empty ground, AnnA stretched out her arms. "I will jump now."

Jimmy Joe, Piper, and Rory Ray waited and watched. AnnA closed her eyes and, in the blink of an eye, disappeared.

Rory Ray started. "Where'd she go?"

Jimmy Joe waved his arm through the space where AnnA had just stood. "What happened? How'd she do that?"

Piper remained still, processing what she had just witnessed. "She jumped," she said, slowly understanding.

"Where?"

"What does that mean?"

"She jumped," Piper repeated. "She's teleporting. Jumping from place to place." Piper moved her hand from one spot to the next in the same way AnnA had just done.

"But where'd she go?"

"And when's she coming back?"

Suddenly, AnnA appeared again. She "jumped" on top of a barrel, almost tumbling off. Piper helped her down.

"AnnA, that's unbelievable! What a great talent." Piper gave AnnA's hand a gentle squeeze of congratulations. "I've never met anyone who was a jumper before! I didn't even know what it was."

"I have much to learn. It is very new," AnnA admitted.

"I'm real glad you came to show me."

The true purpose of AnnA's trip returned to her. "That is not why I am here. Piper, your friends are in trouble. Conrad asked Elder Equilla for help, but she says it is not up to the Chosen Ones to save Outsiders. Elder Equilla says it is time for your friends to stay on Mother Mountain and be with their own kind. But your friends did not wish to stay, so Elder Equilla insisted."

"Insisted?" No matter what Elder Equilla said, Conrad and the others would have wanted to return home; their mission was too vital. "How did she insist?"

AnnA spoke carefully. "Elder Equilla has embraced them."

The difference in words and the language between the Chosen Ones and Outsiders was a frustration to Piper, at that moment more than ever. "What does that mean, AnnA? How does she embrace them?"

"She holds them tight." AnnA wrapped her arms out in front of her like she was hugging something. "She will not let them leave."

Piper slowly allowed the air to leak out of her lungs as AnnA's meaning became clear. "You mean that they're prisoners? Elder Equilla is holding Conrad prisoner?"

AnnA tilted her head to the side. "What is 'prisoner'?"

"It's like a jail. It's . . . They're trapped. Against their will," Piper explained.

"Yes! This is so. Conrad wants to come home, but Elder Equilla will not let him. She keeps them all."

"So Conrad sent you to get me? Because he wants me to free him?" Despite the enormity of such a task, not to mention the impossibility of attempting it, Piper's heart leapt at the idea. Her friends wanted and needed her.

AnnA shook her head. "No."

Piper deflated. "He didn't?"

"Conrad told me not to come. He said it would be too dangerous for you. But I did not listen. I jumped." AnnA was clearly pleased with the fact that she was able to have accomplished such a feat. "I jumped because I think your friends need you."

Tears came to Piper's eyes. "Yes, they do. They need me."

"You can fly to Xanthia and free them."

"Fly?" Piper stopped, her heart sinking. "Didn't Conrad tell you?"

AnnA prepared a space to jump. "You must hurry."

"Hold it, AnnA. Wait." Piper reached out to AnnA. "Conrad didn't tell you?" It was clear from AnnA's face that Conrad had not. "AnnA, I can't fly."

AnnA's smile slid off. "I have seen you fly. Is this Outsider fun?"

Piper could feel her face grow warm, the embarrassment of her flightless state still an open wound. "I can't fly."

"She's not fooling you," Jimmy Joe butted in. "Her feet might as well be glued to the ground."

"You got that right," Rory Ray agreed.

AnnA let go of Piper's hand, trouble tugging at the corner of her mouth. "But if you cannot fly, then you are an Outsider."

Piper's face was now bright red. "I wouldn't say that.

It's like you said: we have to rescue the others." Piper looked to everyone around her. "We could do it. If we all worked together—like a team."

"A team?" Rory Ray raised a skeptical eyebrow.

"Outsiders are not allowed on Mother Mountain," AnnA said unequivocally.

Piper grabbed AnnA's arm. "But if my friends aren't released, a terrible thing will happen."

AnnA faltered. "But . . . how would you be able to do such a thing?"

"We'll work together. All of us."

AnnA looked from Piper to Rory Ray to Jimmy Joe. They were not much to look at.

"Please!" Piper begged. "Will you help us?"

AnnA shook her head.

CHAPTER

28

*J*UMPING TO REACH PIPER HAD COM-
pletely exhausted AnnA's extremely limited sup-
ply of courage. It wasn't that she didn't want to help; it
wasn't that she didn't see the need for it; it was that she
felt overwhelmed at the very thought of it. And there
was much that needed to be thought of.

First of all they had to find a way to get to Xanthia,
which was at the top of a mountain a good distance
away. Once there, they would have to find the others
while at the same time not being noticed. This was also
a difficult task, since the Chosen Ones numbered less
than five hundred and knew each other intimately.

Finally, but most difficult of all, was freeing Piper's
friends and escaping Xanthia.

All this AnnA knew. The fact that Piper was unable
to fly was the unexpected wild card that had blindsided
her and derailed her confidence entirely.

Absolutely none of these things worried Piper. In fact it appeared to AnnA that Piper was strangely energized and boundlessly optimistic.

"Saving people in dire situations is what I do, AnnA." Piper was on her feet, unable to sit or stand still. "I know all about it. I've rescued orphans off buses about to fall into ravines. I've rescued folks off airplanes. I can do this with my eyes closed!"

"And you have done this since you could not fly?"

"Well, no."

"And"—AnnA pointed out haltingly—"all your other friends put together were not able to free themselves, but you are convinced you will be able to even though . . . you are different now?"

Piper waved away the question as though it were no matter at all. "You know what we need? Before every big mission we always have a team meeting. That's what we need to do! Team meeting."

Piper led AnnA into the barn, and once inside, she, like Rory Ray and Jimmy Joe had, stopped in her tracks. Unlike Jimmy Joe and Rory Ray, she had no context or understanding of anything that her eyes fell upon. The strange flashing lights, the hum of the machines, the clicking from Conrad's latest science experiment bubbling away in the loft overhead were equal parts confusing and frightening.

At the meeting table Piper sat AnnA to her right. Jimmy Joe and Rory Ray took the chairs on the other side.

"So," Piper said, realizing that none of them had ever participated in a team meeting and that she had never actually led one. "So, my friends are trapped. Right, AnnA?"

"This is so."

"And the logical thing to do is to bring them home." Piper looked to the others for confirmation on this point. "Do you agree?"

Rory Ray didn't necessarily want more kids like Piper living next door to him, and Jimmy Joe had never much liked them, either. "Agreement" might be too strong a word to describe their feelings on the subject. AnnA really didn't think it was a great idea to try such a thing and certainly didn't think it likely that they could accomplish it.

"Conrad did say to me that he did not want your help," AnnA pointed out.

"Yes, but Elder Equilla has imprisoned him, so now it's up to us." Piper was painfully aware that this was like no other team meeting she had ever participated in. Rapid-fire discussion, ideas flying back and forth, disagreements, compromises, pertinent data, selfless acts of courage, cunning plans—those were the team meetings Piper was used to.

"Listen to me," she said, making a fist and pounding it on the table in what she hoped would rouse those present but came off as feeble and hurt her hand besides. "I'm saying that we're their last hope. They're depending on us. The safety of the world is at stake, and this world is worth fighting for. Who is with me?"

AnnA looked down at her lap. Rory Ray sniffed loudly, and Jimmy Joe took to picking a piece of carrot out of the back of his teeth.

"I'll take your silence as acceptance." Piper sat back down. "Now let's start planning! Ideas?"

Awkward silence.

"Anyone?" Piper leaned forward. "There's no wrong answer."

"I could blow something up," Rory Ray offered, showing his first bit of interest.

AnnA gasped. "Blow up?"

"That's a wrong answer, Rory Ray. We're not blowing anything up." Piper put her hand on AnnA's arm. "I won't let them blow anything up."

"Outsiders do not belong on Mother Mountain," AnnA said, suddenly at her wits' end. "They cannot come. It is forbidden. They are savages."

Rory Ray bristled. "I'm not the one going around in a bedsheet."

"Yeah," Jimmy Joe said. "We'll go if we want to go. You can't tell us what to do."

AnnA's face was tangled in fear and anger. "Outsiders have no thoughts. They kill and do not care. They are without a soul."

"It's okay, AnnA." Piper tried to soothe her. "Calm down."

AnnA had heard the stories. She knew all about Outsiders. She was not going to be calm. "Ugly. Dangerous. Bloodthirsty."

Rory Ray's hackles got higher with each word. "We'll go up there and kick some Chosen One butt," Rory Ray growled. "You can't take our people and get away with it. I'm in. I say we burn the place down."

"No burning, Rory Ray. That is not a good idea." Piper placed her hands up as though she could shield the two sides from each other. "AnnA, we just need to free Conrad and the others. As soon as we do that, we'll leave."

AnnA glowered. "I will not bring such danger to my people."

"Please, AnnA. Look at me." With difficulty AnnA brought her eyes back to Piper. "You have my word that we'll do no harm. You know it's not right what Elder Equilla is doing. You know that they should be allowed to leave. All I'm asking is that you help us get them back. Please."

AnnA sighed. "I have your word?"

"You have my word."

Rory Ray sat back and crossed his arms over his chest, glaring. As the room returned to silence, it occurred to Piper that preventing her team from fighting with each other might be just as difficult as actually saving her friends.

"You know what? Maybe we're the sort of team that doesn't need team meetings," Piper decided. "Or plans. We'll be the sort of team that 'wings it' and flies by the seat of our pants." She got to her feet and clapped her hands together to create a sense of energy and excitement. "So let's go to Xanthia."

"How?" AnnA challenged. "If you cannot fly, you cannot get there."

"Ah! So, so, we'll . . ." Piper flung her arms out and said the first thing that came into her head. "We'll jump!"

AnnA's face drained of all color.

CHAPTER

29

"*I* KNOW WHAT YOU'RE THINKING," PIPER said quickly, "but it's going to be alright. The first time I flew holding someone, I thought I'd drop 'em for sure. We'll give it a test run, and you can get comfortable with it. Trust me, you'll be an old hand at it in no time. It's like riding a bike."

"What is 'bike'?"

Of course AnnA didn't know what a bike was. Piper waved it away. "Forget I said that. It's as easy as pie. You'll see."

A short while later, AnnA stood in the farmyard with Fido in her arms. Fido was thrilled by the attention and alternately licked and wiggled about to encourage more petting. On the ground, Piper had placed two rocks, twenty feet apart. She had AnnA stand at one rock.

"So you just focus on where you want to go and then you jump there. Is that how it works?" Piper said.

AnnA was trembling, her eyes wide. She nodded her head.

"Good." Piper clapped her hands together. "So do it the same way as always, but this time when you do it, you'll take Fido with you. You don't have to jump far, just over to that rock. See?"

AnnA did see.

Piper stood back where Rory Ray and Jimmy Joe were waiting. Together they watched AnnA.

"You think she's gonna be able to do it?" Jimmy Joe spoke quietly.

"What if she jumps and turns that thing she's holding inside out so all its guts spill out?" Rory Ray's face was equal parts disgust and anticipation. As revolting as it would be to see Fido's insides, there was a certain thrill to it. "There'd be blood dripping all over the place. Like an explosion of it!" Rory Ray made a fist and had his fingers spring outward to demonstrate exactly what he meant by explosion.

"Geez Louise, would you keep stuff like that to yourself?" Piper snorted, elbowing Rory Ray in the ribs. "And that's not going to happen. Now shush."

AnnA's chest pumped up and down. She looked to Piper like she might be hyperventilating.

"You're fine, AnnA. Nothing bad will happen. Just go on and close your eyes."

AnnA closed her eyes, got control of her breathing, and . . . disappeared with Fido.

"She jumped!" Jimmy Joe, in his excitement, stated the obvious.

Now all eyes were on the second rock, waiting. "You can do it, AnnA," Piper said under her breath. "Just do it."

The seconds stretched into an uncomfortable length of time. Piper nervously bit her lip, her toe tapping in the dirt.

"It shouldn't take her this long." Jimmy Joe gnawed on his thumbnail. "Fido probably already exploded."

"For sure," Rory Ray agreed.

Piper walked over to the second rock, as though being closer would help the situation. "C'mon, AnnA. C'mon. You can do it. Jump back."

SNAP. AnnA was suddenly directly in front of Piper, only inches away. Piper screamed in surprise. AnnA screamed because Piper screamed. Jimmy Joe, who couldn't see AnnA, screamed because he assumed there was blood. Rory Ray dashed forward into the fray because it was a marine-like thing to do.

When she had recovered from her initial start, Piper looked at AnnA and instantly noticed that she was without Fido.

"What happened? Where's Fido?" Piper touched

AnnA's stomach where she had held Fido, as though somehow he was still there but invisible.

"Did he explode?" Rory Ray wanted to know. "Is there blood?"

"I—I jumped."

"Yes, we saw. But Fido . . ."

AnnA looked confused. "You said to jump with Fido. I jumped with Fido."

"But where is Fido now?"

"Fido is on Mother Mountain," AnnA said slowly.

Piper sagged with relief. "Oh! You jumped home with Fido and then came back here. Oh, I understand. And when you got to Mother Mountain, Fido was . . . he was in one piece?"

"He was in the same piece as he was in before I jumped. Is this not a good thing?" There was no end to how confusing Outsiders were to AnnA.

"Yes, yes of course. You did everything great. But don't you see, AnnA? You can jump with people. It was easy! Right?" Piper clutched AnnA's hands excitedly.

A sunrise of a smile crested AnnA's face. "Yes," she said, "it was easy."

"This means you can take us to Xanthia with you," Piper continued. "We can all jump there."

Rory Ray pumped his fist in the air, giving off a hearty "oorah!"

AnnA recoiled, frightened by this vocal onslaught.

"Stop it, Rory Ray." Piper put her arm over AnnA protectively. "If you're going to come with us, you can't act like that. A Chosen One would never do that."

Rory Ray pulled down his fist.

"Okay," Piper said. "Now for the next part of the plan."

CHAPTER

30

UNTIL PIPER SPOKE HER PLAN, SHE hadn't actually known what it was. She heard herself say that they would arrive on Mother Mountain while the Chosen Ones were still asleep and get to Conrad and the others before anyone knew they were there. She had no idea what they would do once they reached Conrad, but she would think of that when the time came.

It was decided that AnnA would jump them in one at a time. As Rory Ray and Jimmy Joe didn't want to be the first, Piper bravely stepped forward, determined to demonstrate to the others how easy it was going to be.

"What do I do?" Piper waited in front of AnnA.

"I do not know," AnnA whispered back, looking over Piper's shoulder at the boys. "Fido was the first living thing I ever jumped with."

"Let's hold hands," Piper advised. Reaching out,

Piper took hold of AnnA's trembling fingers. "It's okay, AnnA. You can do this."

"I am not so sure."

"Just do what you do."

Puffing out a shaky breath, AnnA closed her eyes. Piper silently said a prayer when all at once her stomach felt like it was dropping down to the ground and her head felt dizzy. She could feel her body dissemble, stretch apart into air, and then just as quickly snap back into place like a rubber band.

"Piper?"

Piper opened her eyes. AnnA was peering at her, an alarmed expression on her face. "You do not look well," AnnA said.

Piper leaned over and threw up. "Ugh," she groaned when she could speak again. "I can't say I thought it would feel like that."

AnnA patted Piper on the back. "It is startling the first time, but you are on Mother Mountain. We are here!"

When AnnA was sure that Piper had finished throwing up, she went back for Jimmy Joe and then Rory Ray. Both of the boys arrived, as Piper did, with a green look to their faces. Jimmy Joe retched into a vine, but Rory Ray, ever the marine, swallowed firmly and punched his fist into his hand.

"Let's do this!" Rory Ray said.

It was not quite dawn when the four of them were safely stashed in a secluded nook off the main plateau on Mother Mountain. The boys, having never been to Xanthia, peeked out to see what they could see.

As the tallest mountain in a remote, vast range, Mother Mountain was an imposing presence in Xanthia. Nestled in her peaks about three quarters of the way up, the Chosen Ones had settled themselves into cliff dwellings that were hollowed out of the mountain in a horseshoe shape. The three tiers of dwellings, with their graceful stone archways, brought to mind Mount Olympus, while the flowering vines that grew on them added the charm of an old English village. To Jimmy Joe, it closely resembled what he thought heaven would look like.

"Man." Jimmy Joe whistled soft and low. "This place is something."

The breaking of the dawn cast a golden glow over the white stones on the mountain, making them appear luminous. Mother Mountain had diverted her waters so that they tumbled down the center divide, pooling on the large plateau at the base of the tiers. From there, the waters gathered before gently flowing over the precipice to the valley below.

"We must hurry. The sun is coming, and the singer

will be out to greet it soon. All will be woken." AnnA set out.

Piper said, "Where are they being kept?"

"I will take you." AnnA led them through a curving passageway to stairs. Rory Ray tried to keep track of the many twists and turns but soon became hopelessly disoriented.

Piper, who had spent some time in Xanthia, already knew about the strange creatures there. Like the messenger squirrels the size of small dogs that mimicked human voices and traveled throughout the mountain as the communication system, being paid for their efforts with nuts. She knew that things were not only beautiful but had a purpose and sometimes a keen intelligence, too. Like the purple flowers on the vines that crawled up the stone, which gave off heat when it was cold and a cool mist in the summer. The banks of gardens were populated with fruit and vegetables not known to Outsiders, bursting with strong flavors. Piper was prepared for all of this, but Jimmy Joe and Rory Ray craned their necks every few steps, unable to believe their eyes.

Soon enough, they emerged on the very top balcony.

"The elders council chamber is just over there." AnnA pointed to the far side of the curving structure, where lights burned and the low rumblings of conversation wafted their way. "We must make like the wind or they will know we are here."

With her flowing robes and bare feet, AnnA made no sound. Taking care, the others attempted to mimic her stealth.

"In here. Hurry!" AnnA guided them into a chamber filled with such dense foliage that to enter the room they had to push it aside to make passage. The draping vines tickled them as they went past, sticking shoots into tender areas of their neck or on their sides. Rory Ray batted them away.

"Stop tickling." Jimmy Joe pushed a vine off his neck.

"It is letting you know that it is watching you," AnnA said.

"What do you mean watching?" Rory Ray was on alert now.

"It is called a guardian vine. It guards." Inside the chamber, the vine was slithering in a seemingly endless riotous coil. The chamber was a round, cavernous room, and in the center of it AnnA came to a stop.

Piper looked about eagerly, seeing nothing but the vine. "So? Where are they?"

AnnA pointed to the ceiling. "Up," she said.

Everyone looked up. The ceiling of the room reached

thirty feet above them. Halfway up, chiseled out of the stone, were crevices, each one the size of a large closet. Each contained a cozy white sleeping mat, a table with a bowl of fruit set out on it, and a jug of water.

A head poked over the edge of one of the nooks: Smitty. "Piper is here!"

Now heads were rising up off sleeping mats, and faces came into view.

"Piper! It's Piper."

"Piper, I'm so glad to see you!"

"How did you get here?"

"Can you get us out?

Last of all, Piper saw Conrad. He had bite marks on his arms and legs and an exhausted, defeated expression on his face.

Myrtle bent over, squinting at the boys. "Who are they?" She pointed at Jimmy Joe and Rory Ray.

"This is Jimmy Joe Miller and his brother Rory Ray."

Once again, Myrtle looked completely confused, but just as Piper was going to explain further, she held up her hand. "Wait. They're the locals from Lowland County? Why would you bring them here?"

"Looks to me like you could do with all the help you can get," Jimmy Joe said with an edge. "And I'm not a local. I'm a . . . resident. A resident of Lowland County."

"Well, c'mon," Piper urged. "We're here to take you

home. Get down from there, and let's get going on our way."

"We can't get down, Piper," Conrad said, his voice weary. "The vine is keeping us prisoner. The minute we try to leave, we're thrown back. Not even Daisy can strong-arm it."

Daisy stepped forward, and the vine shot out, blocking her way. She grabbed it and squeezed, but another vine came out, grabbed her by the scruff of her neck, and tossed her back on her sleeping mat.

"That happens every time," Ahmed said.

"Like clockwork," Nalen agreed.

"But it's just a vine!" Piper couldn't believe this. With all their talents they couldn't figure out how to outwit a vine? Surely not! "Conrad, what's the plan?"

Conrad reached up to his throat, and Piper saw that a silver band had been fastened around it. "Elder Equilla put collars on us," he said.

"The collar is generally used on small children when their abilities first blossom and there is concern that they will hurt themselves," AnnA explained. "Some talents are very powerful and need time to develop and mature slowly. The collar regulates the degree to which you can access your ability."

"Whatever that means." Kimber snorted. "This thing makes us normal."

"Equilla wanted to make sure that we don't get out of here."

"So that collar takes your talent away?" Now it was abundantly clear to Piper why they were stuck and couldn't get out. "Well, there's got to be something we all can do."

"We've gone over it a thousand times," Conrad explained. "We're on a mountain surrounded by people who are extraordinary. Equilla has commanded that we stay, and no one here is going to help us. Chosen Ones are obedient to the elders."

"Equilla wants to make sure we don't stop the bugs," Jasper said.

"But"—Piper clutched her hands together—"there has to be something that can be done! What do I do, Conrad?"

Conrad looked tired, rumpled, and worried. "I had a chance to see my father and mother when we first arrived. Equilla has put them in isolation too until she can be sure they are safe for the Chosen Ones to be around."

"Safe? Why wouldn't they be safe?" Conrad's parents were hardly criminals. His little sister Aletha was six and not likely to cause trouble.

"Any contact Chosen Ones have with Outsiders causes unrest. They start asking questions, and Equilla wants to make sure that isn't encouraged. She doesn't like questions."

"She's also building a wall to keep Outsiders out," Myrtle added.

Lily nodded her head, "And now she doesn't want to let us go, either."

"I think I can see someone coming." Smitty craned his neck to get a better view. "My vision is not that great, but I'm pretty sure someone's heading our way."

AnnA grabbed Piper's arm, pulling her back. "We must hide," she urged.

Jimmy Joe and Rory Ray, taking their cues from Piper, followed closely. AnnA pushed aside the hanging ivy and tucked them behind layers of it until they were shielded completely. Then she snuck in next to them so that she, too, was hidden.

"Make way," said a deep male voice.

Using her fingers to brush aside leaves, Piper was able to create a peephole through the ivy. Between leaves, she could make out ten elders walking into the chamber. Like AnnA, they were clothed in flowing white robes; each robe had its own unique adornment. Last of all to enter was a woman, more regal and silent than the others, her hair as white as her robes, and her eyes the color of steel.

"Who's that?" Jimmy Joe whispered in Piper's ear.

"That's Elder Equilla. She's like the president around here, and the others are in her council. They make all the rules."

Jimmy Joe found her mesmerizing. "She looks like a snow queen."

When she came to the center of the room, standing in front of all the others, Elder Equilla lifted her hand and flicked it with a graceful twist. Instantly, the ivy pulled away from the opening of each child's nook.

"I invite you all to commune with me," Equilla said with a voice like a song.

Tendrils of the vine snapped forward and plucked up the kids, grabbing them by the scruff of their necks and plunking them down in front of the elders. When they had brushed themselves off and settled, Equilla directed her attention to Conrad.

"Asanti." She bowed.

Out of politeness, Conrad returned the bow.

"It is not in our custom to require our people to have 'rest' time. It is not a situation we wish to continue or find sustainable."

"Let's be clear," Conrad said. "We're not resting; we're imprisoned against our will."

Equilla looked around. "But I trust you are comfortable? All your needs are met?"

Conrad could not dispute that. "Yes."

"Then it is also restful. Both may be true at the same time." Elder Equilla folded her hands in front of her. "We understand that you wish to leave us and return to the Outside. We have considered this request and will now offer our decision. It is our belief that like must be with like: that the Chosen Ones are safer and happier with their own kind, so too the Outsiders. It is for this reason that we have invited you to be with us. Even though you have had the misfortune of being born on the Outside, you are Chosen, as we can see by your gifts." Equilla paused to look among the children.

Conrad, with his shining blond hair and sharp blue eyes, didn't take his gaze from her.

"While I cannot understand what calls you back to such a place, I must honor your wish to return." Equilla shook her head as though their ignorance and lack of judgment was not to be understood by a rational mind. "However, it is clear to me that, for your safety and for the peace that now exists between Chosen Ones and Outsiders, clear lines must be drawn. Therefore, if you wish to return to the Outside, then you must be an Outsider. We will assist you in this process."

Equilla nodded to one of her council members, and he stepped forward. "There are those of us who are skilled at releasing unwanted gifts. I assure you it is painless."

Conrad's lips drew into a thin line.

"If you remain with us, then you will remain as you are and enjoy all the privileges and benefits of Mother Mountain. As well, you will abide by the rules of our people, and no Chosen One may leave Mother Mountain or associate with an Outsider. It is forbidden."

"What in the heck is she saying?" Jimmy Joe whispered. "I don't get it."

"Shhh," Piper warned him.

"Under what authority can you impose this upon us?" Conrad addressed the council as a whole.

"You came to our home uninvited," Elder Equilla pointed out. "When you set foot on this mountain, you placed yourself under our authority."

"I do not accept that," Conrad said.

"Your acceptance or lack thereof is incidental. It will be so." Elder Equilla's voice held not a trace of emotion.

"So either we stay and keep our talents but never return home, or you take away our abilities and we get to see our families. And either way you will do nothing to help save the planet."

Equilla bowed her head.

"Ohhhh," Jimmy Joe said. "I get it. Holy cow, that's harsh. D'ya think she'll actually make them normal?"

"In a heartbeat," Piper whispered.

"Today is an important day. Spring has come to

Xanthia, and it is our festival day. There is much to do. I will allow you to rest for this day and consider your choice." Equilla swept away, pausing just as she came to the spot directly in front of where Piper, AnnA, and the boys were hidden. She stood for several breaths, cocking her head slightly as though she could hear them.

Piper held her breath, and AnnA bit her lip. The ivy chose that moment to tickle Rory Ray, and he dug his fingernails into the palm of his hand to stop himself from moving.

"Tonight," Equilla said, "when we give thanks at sunset, I will either introduce you as new, cherished members of Xanthia, or we will allow the community to bid you farewell and perform the ceremony of release. I will await your decision. Asanti."

Equilla flicked her hand, and the ivy vines, which followed her commands, snatched each child up and efficiently deposited them back into their nooks. In the same graceful, quiet way that they had entered, the council flowed out of the chamber after Equilla.

When the coast was clear, Piper burst out of the vines like she had been submerged underwater.

"We've gotta get you out of here!"

CHAPTER

31

No one could figure out how to escape, not even Conrad, even though he pulled at his collar and held his head as though squeezing ideas into his brain. With the collar on, he no longer had boundless intelligence to rely upon.

"There's no way I'm giving up my speed. I'd die if I couldn't run." Myrtle jutted out her chin.

"Same. What would I be without my electricity?" Kimber batted at the ivy closest to her, and it poked back.

"What about the bugs? They'll be blasting soon." Ahmed paced back and forth. He had been put in a nook away from his twin brother. Usually they were within arm's reach of each other, and the distance made him feel vulnerable and shaky.

"Maybe," Violet offered quietly, "some of us will have to give up our gifts to go back to help, and the others will stay here."

"But who's gonna stay, and who'll go? And if we don't have any special abilities, what can we do to help anyway? That just defeats the purpose, and Equilla knows that."

Piper leaned over to AnnA and Rory Ray, who were closest to her. "FYI," she said quietly, "this is what a team meeting is supposed to sound like."

"I thought we were gonna fight something," Rory Ray groused.

"Listen up!" Smitty called out. "They're bringing our breakfast in soon. You'd better disappear if you don't want to end up in one of these."

"Piper, go home," Conrad said. "You can't help us."

"I'm not going anywhere," Piper insisted. "I'll figure something out."

"There is nothing that you can do. Even if you could fly, it wouldn't be enough. It would take a team to break us out of here."

Piper snapped her fingers. "So then I'll just have to get a team of Chosen Ones together who will help us."

Kimber snorted. "Like they'd ever help us."

"AnnA is helping us," Piper pointed out.

"We already asked them," Conrad reminded Piper. "And they already told us no. They don't want anything to do with Outsiders."

A noise in the corridor behind them caught AnnA's

attention, and she grabbed Piper's arm and pulled at her. "This way."

"But—" Piper tried her best to reason through the situation. "Did everyone get to vote on it? Did every Chosen One say no?"

"Of course not." AnnA tugged at her. "It was a decision for the council of elders. We must rely upon their wisdom in all things."

"Uh, did I mention that someone is coming?" Smitty interrupted.

AnnA firmly grabbed Piper's arm and ran. "We'll be back for you," Piper promised. Rory Ray and Jimmy Joe wasted no time in keeping up with her.

"In here." AnnA turned quickly and led them down a small, narrow passage, and then suddenly they were out on the balcony.

Bright morning sunlight was now showering the mountain. Down below, on the edge of the plateau, a tall, thin man was singing the morning song that woke the Chosen Ones and called them to the day. AnnA's eyes shifted back and forth as she rapidly made calculations. "You will be seen," she muttered. "I must get you out of sight. I can't jump you home from here. I will . . . have to take you to my sleeping place."

Bursting into a trot, AnnA tried to appear like she has having a typical morning. It was quickly clear she had no experience in deception of any sort and only succeeded in drawing attention to the group with her uncomfortable display of normalcy.

"What happens if we're caught?" Rory Ray trotted next to her.

"An uninvited Outsider has never been on Mother Mountain," AnnA said. "You would be sent away as soon as possible."

That seemed logical to Jimmy Joe. "So they'd send us on back home?"

"Or throw you off the mountain," AnnA said. "Most likely that, but it is difficult to know."

Rory Ray and Jimmy Joe looked down. They were a long, long way from the ground, and the valley below the mountain didn't exactly look like a safe place to be. They both made a mental note to do whatever it took not to get thrown off the mountain.

As AnnA guided the group through Mother Mountain's corridors and stairways, Chosen Ones began to appear, each presenting the potential threat of discovery. At times, AnnA shielded them or quickly pushed them into a nook until the Chosen One passed. It was in a nook, while they were all attempting to look nonchalant, that Jimmy Joe peeked out at the passing Chosen One and saw to his surprise that if he hadn't been wearing a robe, he wouldn't have looked out of place in Lowland County.

"Why do they hate us so much?" Jimmy Joe whispered. "I don't get it."

"A long time ago, when Chosen Ones and Outsiders lived together, the Outsiders hunted the Chosen Ones down," AnnA said, careful to keep her voice low. "If the Chosen Ones hadn't fled to Xanthia, we wouldn't have survived."

"I've never heard anything about that," Rory Ray said. "How come we don't know about it?"

"It is best that the Outsiders forget about us so that we are safe. Chosen Ones must not forget, and we are taught the histories by our storytellers so we will be safe." Seeing that the coast was clear, AnnA once again guided the group out, keeping her eyes peeled for other possible threats. At last, AnnA hurried them into her chamber, and the four of them came face-to-face with a woman who looked like AnnA but thirty years or so older.

AnnA's mother, HannAh, was graceful, her red hair mellowed to a copper shine and artfully coiled around the top of her head with flowers tucked in it. She was holding a dress out in front of her when the children came rushing in but was so startled by their sudden appearance she dropped the dress and yelped, covering her face with her hands.

"Maman," AnnA began. "It is Piper. You remember Piper."

HannAh could not focus on Piper because she was pointing at Jimmy Joe and Rory Ray—two faces she had never seen before. Everyone in Xanthia knew everyone else, and these two boys were not from Xanthia, which meant they were not Chosen Ones.

Next, she looked to AnnA for an explanation.

Her mother had met Piper before, and this seemed like a good place to start. "She needed my help, and these boys—they are her friends. And they are not bad. They will not do violence. They have given their word."

"What value is the word of an Outsider?"

"They come in peace."

"It is forbidden!" HannAh was clutching AnnA now, pulling her away from the Outsiders.

"But, Maman . . ."

"They are not safe."

AnnA knew it would be difficult to get her mother to understand. She, like all Chosen Ones, would never believe that the Outsiders were safe. Anna had to find another way to get her mother to look at them differently. "They are hungry, Maman."

"Hungry?" HannAh looked over AnnA's shoulder at

the group. They did indeed look hungry, particularly the two boys.

"Their bellies ache," AnnA continued softly. "I do not want them to starve. It makes me . . . sad."

It was easy for HannAh to believe that Outsiders would let their children go hungry. "Chosen Ones do not starve children," HannAh agreed. "They must eat."

After that, HannAh hurried them over to a low table, around which were arranged pillows and soft rugs. AnnA was sent out and returned with several steaming bowls of food. The first dish looked like pasta but turned out to taste like cinnamon porridge. The next one had nuts and berries, and the last was crunchy and salty. The food was served with a steaming red tea.

Jimmy Joe and Rory Ray ate as though they had never eaten before. The food was so good, and they had appetites like bottomless pits, despite the fact that they were regularly fed.

"Thank you, ma'am," Jimmy Joe said, shoving food into his face.

"Best grub we've ever had." Rory Ray had smears of it on his cheek and chin.

HannAh could not eat a bite and sat, watching them. "They look dangerous," she said to AnnA in a quiet voice.

"Maman, no." AnnA colored with embarrassment.

HannAh persisted. "You must take care." Outside, a

loud horn sounded, and HannAh looked up. "The festival call. I will be missed if I do not go."

On festival days, all were needed, and in such a small community, if someone did not appear, they would be looked for. HannAh was torn between her duty and her need to protect AnnA, and her face quivered with the dilemma. "If they come for me, they will find the Outsiders here."

"Go," AnnA said to her mother.

HannAh glared at Jimmy Joe and Rory Ray. "I know what is in your hearts," she said softly but with venom. "You are not welcome."

Jimmy Joe and Rory Ray looked down at their laps. Jimmy Joe in particular had a hurt, confused look on his face. He felt the urge to apologize but didn't know what for or how to do it.

"Maman." AnnA helped her mother up and toward the door. "Go."

"Walk with me," HannAh urged, taking AnnA's hand and pulling her onto the balcony.

Reluctantly, AnnA went with her mother, shooting a parting glance back. When the two of them were gone, Piper and the boys released the air in their lungs in a loud whoosh.

"No offense," Rory Ray snorted, "but these Chosen Ones need to let the past go."

Piper sprang up from the table and tucked herself back into the shadows by the doorway so that she could not be seen while she peeked outside.

Jimmy Joe ate the last of his meal thoughtfully. "She sure seems a little . . . unfriendly."

Piper snorted. "You think your ma and pa were glad to have me at your house? You think they were friendly and welcoming?"

"That's different." Rory Ray crossed his arms across his chest. "They've got good reason for it."

"Oh yeah?" Piper said. "And what's that?"

Rory Ray swung out his arm at Piper like it should be obvious. He even started to open his mouth with the words "not right in the head" at the front of his tongue but then closed it again. Did he believe that?

Jimmy Joe took a hard swallow.

Piper could see HannAh talking firmly to AnnA a few yards away and, beyond them, the excitement of festival day. Chosen Ones were emerging dressed in fancy robes; the younger girls had ribbons threaded through their hair so that they hung down over their faces. Piper tried to look for other Chosen Ones she knew from the last time she had visited, but it was hard to see their faces through the ribbons.

All at once, an idea came to Piper. Rushing across the chamber, she retrieved the robe that HannAh had dropped to the floor. Just as Piper suspected, it was for AnnA, who was her size. Holding it up against her body, she was relieved to see it was a perfect fit.

"Hurry up," she said to Rory Ray and Jimmy Joe. "I've got a plan. We're moving out."

CHAPTER

32

"*I*'M NOT SO SURE THIS IS A GOOD PLAN."
Rory Ray fussed with the leaf crown on his head
and the flowing robes that were a little bit too tight
across his chest. The three of them were crouched in a
stairway.

Piper had wound herself up in AnnA's dress and then
scrounged robes for the boys to wear. Fortunately, the
spring festival attire had the girls wearing an abundance
of ribbons, and Piper arranged hers so that they covered
her face. She'd also plucked leaves from the climbing
vines and created little masks and crowns that covered
half of the boys' faces. Thankfully, the Chosen boys on
the mountain were wearing them too, so the Millers fit
right in.

No sooner were they dressed than Piper hustled
them out of the chamber in the opposite direction from
where HannAh had spoken with AnnA. Piper's plan,

such as it was, was to return to Conrad and bust him out. How she was going to accomplish that particular feat she couldn't exactly say, but she was taking it one step at a time. Alas, once they rounded their first corner and climbed their first stairway, they were promptly lost.

"I think it's left." Jimmy Joe pointed down a small corridor.

"You don't know what you're talking about, you numbskull; it's right." Rory Ray gave Jimmy Joe a conk on the head. A passing Chosen One, seeing the hit, was shocked by its violent nature and stopped dead in his tracks.

Piper forced a laugh and said loudly, "That is very fun," hitting herself on the head in the same way, then laughing even louder. When the Chosen One moved on, she gave Rory Ray the eye. "Do you want to get us thrown off the mountain?"

Rory Ray shook his head contritely. "Sorry."

Creeping up a staircase tucked off to the side, the three of them climbed to the third tier and found themselves on an overlook to the plateau below, where they were able to see a great commotion by the pooling waters on the main level.

"They're here! They're here!" A cry echoed from all parts of the mountain.

Thinking that they had been discovered, Piper braced herself for the worst when a child raced up to her. "Hurry, or you will miss it!" The child grabbed Piper's hand and pulled her along.

Piper soon found that she was swept up in a stampede of rushing children.

"Have you seen them?" a boy close to Piper yelled out.

"They are flying fast. We must hurry!" another child answered.

As soon as they reached the bottom level by the pooling waters, the rush continued past the Celebration Center and only ended when to go any farther meant they would fall down to the valley below. At the edge, they leaned out dangerously.

"Do you see?"

"Look! Over there!"

"I see! I see!"

Piper looked where fingers were pointing and was able to make out a small group of very small birds in the distance. Someone squeezed up next to her and took her arm. It was AnnA, her face red and her eyes flashing.

"Why did you run away? You must stay with me."

"I wanted to get back to my friends."

AnnA sighed. "If you are discovered?"

"I won't tell on you, AnnA."

Rory Ray and Jimmy Joe joined them. "What's going on? What's everyone looking at?" Jimmy Joe placed a hand above his eyes to shield them from the glare of the morning sun.

"It is spring," AnnA said just loud enough so that they could hear. "On the first day of spring, the Fortune Fliers return home to their nest at the top of Mother Mountain."

Jimmy Joe squinted. "What the heck is a Fortune Flier?"

AnnA had to think of the best way to describe them. "They are . . . Fortune Fliers. If you are able to catch one in your hand, they will whisper your future to you."

"Shut the front door!" Jimmy Joe looked from AnnA to the small, approaching birds in the sky. "You mean they can see the future? No way!"

"We all try to catch them," AnnA said. "That is why there is so much excitement."

The competitive streak in Rory Ray bubbled to the surface. "I'll catch one. No problem."

AnnA did not think so. "It has been generations since the last Fortune Flier was caught. It is very difficult."

Rory Ray snorted. "Not for me."

"I'm better at catching," Jimmy Joe said.

"You couldn't catch a cold." Rory Ray elbowed Jimmy Joe back, and Jimmy Joe jostled him in return.

"Guys," Piper said with an edge to her tone, "I think we've got other things to worry about."

"Look! Look!" children shouted. The Fortune Fliers were now coming into view.

With bodies no bigger than a thumb and a wingspan the size of a melon, the Fortune Fliers clothed themselves in vivid colors of violet, indigo, scarlet, and sage. They were buzzing in swirling patterns that created streaks of bold color in the air. It was said that the Fortune Fliers were the product of a union between a pixie and a mermaid; they sported a pixie face atop a scaly body held aloft by gossamer wings.

Hanley, a boy about the size of Rory Ray who was at the front of the group, hung over the precipice dangerously, then suddenly turned. "To the ledge," he shouted.

Instantly, everyone ran for the ledge.

Because it was Mother Mountain, and because the Chosen Ones were the Chosen Ones, the stampede for the ledge took on its own unique quality. Hanley stretched his body like it was made of taffy. A girl with golden hair named Priscilla was followed by a swarm of bees, and a toddler strobed like a little sun as she ran.

Up ahead, the older and the faster ones were already climbing the rocks behind the waterfall to reach a ledge that jutted out and presented a perfect jumping-off point. The younger ones were doing their best to climb too but mainly fell and landed in the waters and then got out and tried again.

The messenger squirrels were scampering excitedly about and saying the words "Fortune Flier" over and over again, which in turn was drawing the elders to the pooling waters to watch and cheer. Meanwhile, the Fortune Fliers were following the path of the water up to the top of the mountain and had just started to fly up along the waterfall.

Piper and AnnA kept close to the other kids so as not to draw attention to themselves. Piper had the perfect vantage of Rory Ray and Jimmy Joe on the ledge above.

"I have one! Here I go!" Hanley leaned off the ledge as only an elasticated boy could do.

Piper shook her head at the sight of him. "It's an amazing thing to see," she mused, "all the special abilities y'all have."

AnnA agreed distractedly. "We are capable of great things."

"Obviously," Piper sighed, and then stopped dead, her mouth opening. "AnnA! What do all the youngens here think about what's going on with the Outsiders?"

"They do not know of it. The elders do not wish to concern us with these matters, and we are not welcomed at the council meetings."

"But wouldn't the kids here want to help us out? I

mean, if they knew about the bugs and how bad it could get?"

AnnA wrinkled her nose as she thought about this. "We have been taught about the Outsiders through the storytellers. No Chosen One, old or young, wishes to be near them."

"But what if the stories aren't true? Or at least not true anymore," Piper said. "Do you think I'm dangerous?"

"Of course not."

"But I'm an Outsider now."

"No. Well . . . yes, but no." AnnA shook her head and then nodded it and shook it again. "You are different."

"But I'm not different. I have no special ability, and that makes me an Outsider. Am I worth saving?"

"Yes."

"What if all the others are like me?"

AnnA could not wrap her mind around this. "They are Outsiders."

"Oh, AnnA," Piper breathed, grabbing her hand and squeezing it. "I think I have a plan. Can you gather together a handful of kids about our age and just let me talk to them? If I could talk to them, I know I could make them understand."

Before AnnA could answer, a cheer rose from the children above. Hanley had leapt out, bursting through the waterfall and startling the lead Fortune Flier as it flew up.

The Flier was darting and strong, dipping in and out of the water. Flanking him on either side were Fliers with dark purple wings and thick green bodies.

The little birds were not particularly upset when Hanley was suddenly in the middle of them. With adept skill they dodged his grasp and darted around him, giving him a nip on the rear end.

Now kids were leaping in bunches, stretching out their little bodies and waving their arms to grab and grasp. Fortune Fliers buzzed back and forth like angry bees, bearing their sharp teeth. Below, parents cheered and clapped, the noise echoing off the mountain walls amplifying it.

Piper watched Rory Ray thrust his muscular arms about, like a bear trying to take flight. He did his best to snatch a Flier but, like the others, quickly fell into the water below, empty-handed.

One by one they all jumped, until at last the only one left on the ledge was Jimmy Joe, frozen in place. Piper wondered if he'd lost his nerve or perhaps was afraid of heights.

Unbeknownst to Piper, Jimmy Joe had carefully selected a soft pink Flier with wings the color of a purple sunset that had lagged behind the rest. She was graceful and elegant, slowing down to let her tiny little fingers tickle the flowing waters before she began her ascent.

Jimmy Joe kept his eyes locked on her. He did not rush but waited and watched patiently as she approached.

Every Chosen One on the entire mountain was now gathered, their eyes resting on Jimmy Joe.

"I do not know that child," a mother said to another. "Is that Ephram?"

The other mother could not tell. "Whoever he may be, let him catch it."

The pink Flier arched her back and raised her gaze to the top of the mountain, climbing. Jimmy Joe crouched down as she approached, and although his body was in Xanthia, a record inside his mind was playing an old tune, the words to which had been etched onto his brain. *You can't do it, Jimmy Joe. You're too small. We don't want you around, Jimmy Joe. You're a pest.*

How many times had he heard Rory Ray or his other brothers say that to him? He didn't know a number high enough.

The fire in Jimmy Joe's belly flamed up.

He waited for just the right moment and sprang with the grace and stealth of a jungle cat, his hand outstretched, his body lean and reaching.

The delicate pink Flier was not startled by Jimmy Joe's sudden appearance. The purple wings fluttered against his fingertips, the delicacy of the tiny body flitting by the palm of his hand.

From the ground below, Piper watched Jimmy Joe leap and saw him gliding through the air in the perfect trajectory to intercept the Fortune Flier. And then, when his hand was out, the Fortune Flier hovering not more than an inch above, Piper watched and waited for gravity to take Jimmy Joe and pull him down. But gravity did not do that. Gravity forgot all about Jimmy Joe.

For two or perhaps three seconds, Jimmy Joe hovered in the sky. He was flying!

Piper gasped at the sight.

The little Fortune Flier paused to wonder at the boy. That was all the time Jimmy Joe required to close his hand around her.

Jimmy Joe caught the last Fortune Flier.

And then gravity remembered all about him.

Jimmy Joe tumbled down, landing with a loud splash in the waters below. Rory Ray dove at him, lifting him up. Jimmy Joe raised his closed fist.

"I caught it!" he shouted. "I caught a Fortune Flier."

After that every single person on Mother Mountain went bananas.

CHAPTER

33

*J*IMMY JOE WAS HOISTED UPON SHOUL-
ders. Chosen Ones opened their mouths and let out
such cries of triumph, followed by cheering and wild clap-
ping, that Mother Mountain shook. Musicians picked up
their instruments and played heartily, and a wildly happy
song sprang to the lips of all. To catch a Fortune Flier
was an omen of good tiding, a sign of happy things to
come. The older and wiser Chosen Ones rejoiced that
they had lived to see the day. What good fortune!

In all the excitement, Rory Ray got his hands on his
brother and threw him up into the air and let out such a
holler of "oorah" that if there hadn't already been deaf-
ening noise from all around, the Chosen Ones would
surely have crouched and shrunk away in fear.

Jimmy Joe was careful to keep his hands cupped
around the Fortune Flier and not hurt it, even as he was

clapped and congratulated and celebrated. At last, he was the fastest, the strongest, and the smartest.

"What shall you ask? What question do you need to know the answer to?" was asked over and over again.

In the crush of it all, Piper and AnnA came to Jimmy Joe's side, pulling him away. Rory Ray, seeing what they were about, ran interference, creating a path for them to pass through. In the gleeful shouting and uproarious excitement, Jimmy Joe slipped out. The Chosen Ones were so swept away by the magnitude of the moment that the absence of the source of it hardly mattered, and the music and singing turned to dancing, and then the storyteller came forth and relayed the stories of the last Fortune Fliers who had been caught and the fortunes that they had told all those years ago.

While all this was happening and the morning became afternoon, AnnA quietly invited one, then two children, and then more, back to her sleeping place. "Come and see the Fortune Flier," she said to coax them.

Piper had instructed AnnA to select a handful of the best kids, meaning those with the most unique and developed talents. For while it was true that every-one born on Mother Mountain had a gift, not all gifts were equal. Selpeth was yet to do more than make his hair grow faster; Deirdra was born without a shadow, for which no one could think of a single practical use; and Raymal had toes and fingers that were all of equal length but did nothing else besides, which was a great disappointment to him and his family.

AnnA did not invite these to join in the group but instead asked Asher, who could stop time for several seconds, and Kayla, who had the sleeping talent, and her sister Mayla, who had an icy breath. As well, there were Irma, who had the breath of life, and Crona, who could call water. Delia, who was a grower, came last, and like the others, arrived eagerly, unsuspecting of the true nature of the meeting.

When the group was at last gathered and bursting with anticipation to see the Fortune Flier, AnnA quickly explained that Piper had invited two of her Outsider friends to join them. While this news was met with shock and concern, the children were able to temporarily put aside their prejudices lest they miss out on hearing what the Fortune Flier had to say.

"May I see?" Kayla put her eyes to the cracks in Jimmy Joe's hands to peep in.

"Gather, gather—all will see," AnnA said, urging them to come forward and sit close. "But first, Piper would speak with you."

"Asanti." Piper placed her hands together and bowed.

"Asanti," they returned.

"I've come with news." Piper kept her voice even and looked into their eyes so that she could create a connection. She was aware that she must choose her words carefully so as not to startle them. "There are creatures that need your help. They're in pain and they're suffering, and if we don't help them, bad things will happen."

Hanley nodded. "I have heard whisperings of this."

"Yes," Mayla agreed. "My father says that it is an Outsider problem."

"We must not interfere in Outsider business."

"The Outsiders must look after themselves."

"But"—Piper raised her hand to stanch the flow of comments—"what if the Outsiders are not able to help themselves this time? What if only Chosen Ones can do this?"

The Chosen Ones present did not know what to think about this. Piper shot a hopeful glance AnnA's way, but AnnA raised her eyebrow, withholding judgment until the outcome was settled.

"And what if you could use your talents, and by using them, you would help many people?"

Hanley was the first to speak up again. "Which people? Chosen Ones or Outsiders?"

"Well . . ." Piper hesitated, formulating her answer. "I guess you could say it would help the planet. I mean, mainly Outsiders will be affected by it."

"And Chosen Ones?"

Piper nodded her head and shook it at the same time. "Not so much."

AnnA could see the children shift, shaking their heads and murmuring.

"This is a matter for the elders to decide," one of them said.

"Yes," Asher agreed. "What do the elders say? They are wise in all things."

Piper took a deep breath and saw that AnnA was biting her lip; this was going exactly as AnnA had predicted. "Sometimes elders know things, but sometimes they don't," Piper reasoned. "Sometimes you have to make decisions for yourself based on your own information."

Hanley's mouth twisted up. "Why?"

"Because . . . because"—Piper's hands waved in the air as she conjured the answer—"information is power, and because it's important to have all the facts. Because sometimes things change, but people don't, and then we have to be the ones to be the change. D'ya know what I mean?"

Blank expressions and silence.

Piper scratched her head, pushing back a strand of hair that limply dangled against her cheek and fixing her gold lily pin in place. "I know y'all think that the

Outsiders are violent and not worth anything," Piper continued, "and I'm not gonna say they're all good—'cause they're not—but they're not all bad, either. I just think that if we all got to know each other, everything would be better for everyone. I think you can learn stuff from them, and I know we can learn stuff from you." Piper opened her hands and threaded her fingers together like puzzle pieces. "I think we all want the same things, and we'd be stronger and happier if we knew more about each other." She took a deep breath and blew it out. "All I'm saying is that you should see for yourself and make up your own mind."

"But I like being with my own kind," Kayla offered quietly. "I don't want to get to know the Outsiders. They might hurt me. I like it where I am now."

"Me too."

Heads bobbed up and down in agreement. Piper released her clasped hands and sighed. She didn't blame the Chosen Ones; what reason did they have to doubt what their parents and elders had told them, and what purpose could there be to helping those whom they had been taught to hate? Even Jimmy Joe and Rory Ray wouldn't give her the time of day at first and only recently would consider the possibility that she might not be so strange. In the battle between saving the world and opening people's minds, opening their minds was by far the harder task.

"What good ever came of the Outsiders?" Kayla whispered to her sister just loudly enough for Piper to hear. "They cannot do anything."

"But don't you see?" Piper jumped in, pointing her finger at Kayla excitedly. "It was an Outsider who caught the Fortune Flier, not a Chosen One. Jimmy Joe has no ability, or at least not a special ability like y'all have, and yet he did it."

"That is true," Mayla said slowly. "Even Hanley could not catch a Flier."

The creases on their brows softened.

"But if an Outsider who does not have any ability can do great things, then . . ." It took much effort for Hanley to pull the pieces together in his head. "Then does that mean they are better than us?"

"No," Piper said. "That's just it: no one is better."

The Chosen Ones in the room were puzzling over this quietly when Jimmy Joe jumped to his feet, his face popping. "The Fortune Flier is talking. I can hear it!"

Piper ran to him, followed by the rest of the kids, who clustered as closely to Jimmy Joe as they could get, pushing their ears eagerly inward. Jimmy Joe opened his fingers and leaned down. The little bird hopped about his hands and chirped in a lyrical, singsong voice.

"*Gather, gather and listen well,*" the Fortune Flier began.

"Jimmy Joe Miller is plagued by fear,
The voices of others ring in his ear.
He doubts himself and wonders what to do,
Passively watching others paddle his canoe.
Jimmy Joe Miller! Jimmy Joe Miller!
I could see right from the start
There is great courage in his heart.
He has a destiny, but he has a choice.
It is in his power to use his voice
To join and unite, to start the fight
That will ignite the light in this dark night.
There is a new world waiting to be made,
But only if Jimmy Joe Miller isn't afraid.
Jimmy Joe Miller, Jimmy Joe Miller.
What will become of Jimmy Joe Miller?
The answer to that is up to Jimmy Joe Miller."

Finished with her song, the Fortune Flier fluffed her feathers. Jimmy Joe softly exhaled the breath he had been holding.

"I do not understand," AnnA said tentatively. "What do you think it means?"

"Ask it a question," Rory Ray demanded, nudging Jimmy Joe roughly. "Find out if you'll play pro baseball."

"It means," Jimmy Joe began, straightening up, "that

we are destined, all of us, to work together and to stop the bugs."

Rory Ray snorted and rolled his eyes like he was dealing with an imbecile. "You think that's what it means?"

"Yes!" Jimmy Joe glared at Rory Ray. "That's *exactly* what it means. I'm the one who caught the Fortune Flier, so I know. The Fortune Flier said that I know what is in my heart, and that is what it is in my heart. AnnA said the Fortune Fliers are never wrong."

A smile crested Piper's lips.

"And stop telling me what to do, Rory Ray," Jimmy Joe hissed at his brother.

Rory Ray held up his hands. "Okay, okay. Calm down."

Taking flight, the Fortune Flier zipped upward, first completing a full circle around the group and then darting out of the chamber and away.

Hanley scratched his head. "So the Fortune Flier says that we are to go with you? If that is so, what happens now?"

Piper stepped forward. "Now we bust the others out and get out of here!"

"You mean leave Mother Mountain and go to the Outside?" Kayla's face turned as white as a sheet.

Mayla shook her head at the thought. "The Outsiders will murder us!"

"It's not what you've been told," Piper said. "You must see for yourselves and make up your own minds. The Fortune Flier has predicted it."

"And the Fortune Flier is never wrong," AnnA added pointedly.

Piper tried to ignore the look of panicked horror on the faces of Hanley and Irma as she rushed them out of the chamber before they could change their minds.

CHAPTER

34

$\mathcal{A}$S DARKNESS SETTLED INTO THEIR chamber, the sounds of the festival wafted through the air, and with them came bright blue bugs that gave off a flickering light. Conrad paced back and forth in his nook, clawing at his collar. Across from him, he could see Kimber nervously touching the tips of her fingers together.

Smitty was leaning out of his nook, squinting. All at once he put his fists over his eye sockets and pressed down. "It's like I'm blind. I couldn't stand to live like this."

"I'd sacrifice just about anything to get my running back."

"Same."

Ahmed punched at a vine. "I'd be nothing if I couldn't start a thunderstorm."

Ahmed's words struck Conrad. Piper had said almost

the same thing when they had been on the roof of the house. Conrad remembered the look on her face: fragile and helpless. Just like he was feeling right now. A sense of shame and regret crept into his heart. He had wanted to protect Piper, but in the name of concern and caring, he actually hadn't been a very good friend. Regardless of what happened, Conrad wanted to be a good friend to Piper most of all, he decided. He hoped he would be given a second chance. As the minutes slowly dripped past, it seemed as though that was less and less likely.

"The cavalry has arrived," Rory Ray shouted, cutting a figure in the middle of the group. "Oorah!" He raised his fist.

Leaning dangerously out of their nooks, the kids were met with the sight of Piper, Jimmy Joe, and Rory Ray looking up at them. They were joined by AnnA and an assorted group of Chosen Ones. While Piper and the other Outsiders looked defiant and full of fight, the Chosen Ones appeared frightened and tentative, not sure what they were doing.

"We are going to get you out of here!" Piper announced confidently, then lowered her voice and turned to AnnA. "How do you tell the vine to bring them down?"

AnnA said, "Delia is a grower. She would know."

Delia seemed startled to find so many eyes suddenly upon her. She had a riotous mass of jet-black hair threaded with flowers, which she tugged at nervously. "The v–vine," she stuttered, "only answers to Elder Equilla. It will not listen to me."

"Can you try to reason with it?" Piper led Delia to the vine, and she began stroking it.

"I will do what I can," Delia said, but her voice lacked confidence.

"What about these collars?" Conrad called down. "If you could get the collars off, we can do the rest."

"The collars are sealed by Elder Mustanza," AnnA explained. "Only he can release them."

"I could blow them off!" Rory Ray offered.

"True," Piper agreed, "but then they wouldn't have heads, and I think they might miss them."

Rory Ray shrugged off such a small detail.

"Who has a metal gift?" Piper posed to the group. "Can we cut them or slice them off?"

A great cheer rose from the plateau outside, and the sound reverberated throughout the chamber. "Piper," Smitty called down. "The sun has set. Elder Equilla will be on her way."

"The vine will not listen to me," Delia whimpered. "I have asked it and asked it, but it is very stubborn."

"There has to be a way," Piper insisted. "Who else has a talent that will release them?"

The Chosen Ones looked about helplessly.

"What's your ability, again?" Piper asked quickly, pointing to a stocky boy with gray eyes.

"I am Crona. I call water."

Piper didn't completely understand what that was but didn't see any help in it with the current situation, and so she pointed to the girl next to her.

"I am Kayla, and I have the sleeping talent."

"What's that?"

"Kayla can place anyone into a deep sleep," AnnA explained.

Piper snapped her fingers. "Couldn't you put the vine to sleep?"

The solution was so simple it startled the group into a momentary stunned silence.

"I can ask it to sleep," Kayla admitted.

"Great! Do it! Hurry." Piper directed Kayla to the closest tendril. "Now we have to find a way to get them down."

Without waiting for further directions, Hanley stretched his legs up and rose into the air, coming to the crevice where Lily was waiting. The vine was already growing sleepy, curling its leaves in on themselves.

"I can bring you down," Hanley whispered to Lily so as not to wake the vine. Lily arranged her dress in preparation for the journey.

"Mind my hair," she instructed Hanley primly.

Hanley scooped Lily up and gently brought her to the ground, going back for Daisy.

As soon as Lily's feet touched down, Piper closely examined the metal collar around her neck. Lily stretched her neck out and allowed Piper to poke and prod it. "How did they get this thing on you?"

"An elder just clipped it on." Lily snapped her fingers. "Fast. Just like that."

"I can't see very well," Smitty called out from above, "but someone's definitely heading our way."

"Why don't I jump Lily back to your home?" AnnA offered.

"Good idea!" Piper agreed.

A moment after AnnA took Lily's hands, they disappeared into thin air. Hanley placed Conrad's feet on the ground and went back for Daisy. Things were happening fast now and Conrad was anxious to get them moving even faster. "AnnA won't have enough time to jump all of us out. We'll have to get out on foot. Who knows the best way to the tunnel?"

Once again, the Chosen Ones were dumbfounded. "But the tunnel to the Outsider world is on the other side of the valley, and it is forbidden to leave Mother Mountain," Crona said.

"We're going to be breaking some rules today," Conrad pointed out. "You'll have to get used to that."

While the Chosen Ones reluctantly decided on the best route to take, AnnA returned and jumped Jasper out, and Hanley brought Smitty to the ground.

Conrad pulled at his collar, his face red with frustration. "I'm useless with this collar on."

"You'll hurt yourself if you keep doing that," Piper said. "And someone really smart once told me that you don't have to have a superpower to be super powerful. Just do your best—that's what I'm doing."

No sooner were the words out of Piper's mouth than she was suddenly struck by a cramp in her stomach so strong she doubled over and wrapped her arms around her middle. "Ohhh."

"What's wrong?" Conrad reached down to keep her from falling over. The rest of the kids stopped what they were doing to see what was the matter.

"I have a pain in my stomach," Piper moaned.

Conrad looked through the group. "Where's Jasper?"

"AnnA just jumped him out," Smitty reported. "Plus, he couldn't have healed her while wearing that collar."

Conrad shook his head, his frustration returning anew. He had to think!

Piper groaned again, louder this time, and looked down at her belly, where a bright red light was starting to throb. "Conrad, look! It's happening again."

Even with his limited intelligence, Conrad knew

what this meant. "The bugs are preparing to blow. We don't have much time."

Kayla and Mayla stepped forward. "We know a path that will lead us out."

Grabbing Piper's arm to help her, Conrad urged them on. "Let's go! Go!"

As the burning in her stomach grew and the red light throbbed dangerously, Piper's breath came in pants. Without the support of Conrad on one side and Jimmy Joe on the other, she wouldn't have been able to walk at all. She was unaware that she was groaning loudly until Conrad bent down and whispered in an urgent, hushed voice that she must try to be quiet or they would be caught. Before she knew it, she was being handed into a floating raft made more of energy than matter and they were launching out over the valley to the mountain where the mouth of the tunnel could be reached.

Piper could feel the pain inside her brewing and burning. She felt her insides squeezing together like they were trying to pull her into herself. She closed her eyes and, with gritted teeth, used all her energy to withstand it.

CHAPTER

35

As ELDER EQUILLA STOOD ON THE balcony of the council chambers overlooking the festivities below, a breeze came off Mother Mountain, traveled across the stone floor, and rose to her, pulling at her robes.

Equilla breathed in the breeze, holding it in her lungs.

Elder HaSim approached from behind, halting a respectful distance away, his hands clasped in front of his chest, his head bowed.

"They've escaped," Equilla said simply, sighing out the wind.

"Yes." There was a pant to HaSim's voice; he had run a great distance to deliver this news.

"But there is more." Equilla turned, directing her full attention to HaSim. "What is it?"

"They have taken our own with them—young ones, our most powerful and promising." Elder HaSim raised his arm and pointed across the valley. "They enter the caves as I speak."

Equilla blinked twice. "Chosen Ones willingly joining with Outsiders? Leaving Mother Mountain?"

Another breeze approached and wrapped itself around Equilla, twirling about her robes this time, plucking them. Equilla flicked it away.

"I—I cannot account for it," HaSim continued. "The Outsiders must have tricked them or forced them."

"No, they leave willingly. There is more to it." Equilla placed her hands together, creating a steeple with her two pointer fingers and then pressing them to her lips. "One of them has summoned the winds of change; I can feel them swirling at the top of Mother Mountain and gathering force. This is the doing of Piper McCloud. She has called the wind, and it has answered."

"You mean the flier? I heard tell that she is no longer in the sky."

"But the sky is still within her."

Elder HaSim considered the implications. "She is inciting rebellion."

"She talks of a new world order, of unity between the peoples. She thinks it is possible."

Both of them shook their heads at the same time at the impossibility of such a thing. HaSim stated the obvious. "She must be stopped."

"Piper McCloud will not stop, and they will follow her wherever she leads them." Equilla probed the situation, considering all the different aspects. "No, we must pressure a weaker mind, someone who lacks courage and conviction. Why wrestle with the wind when the weakest link will snap under the slightest pressure? Leave it to me."

Elder HaSim bowed to Equilla's greater wisdom. "The races must be kept separate for all our sakes."

"It will be so." Equilla bowed. "Asanti."

"Asanti," HaSim replied.

CHAPTER

36

*T*HE CHILDREN MOVED AS A GROUP, STAYING close together as they cut through the bowels of the mountain. The tunnels were endless, dark, twisty things that went up, up, up and then sharply down. There were sudden turns and unexpected cavernous chambers, and once, the tunnel became little more than a crawl space. Around every corner was a junction, and the right path had to be painstakingly chosen at the risk of being lost in the maze of darkness.

It was hard work for Jimmy Joe to hold Piper up. Unconscious, she let out sharp unexpected groans from time to time, and her midsection throbbed with the red light. Once or twice she woke, and then she would look up at Jimmy Joe and, despite being the one in the greatest danger, reached out to comfort him.

"Don't worry, Jimmy Joe," she said. "We'll get out of there. We've been in worse scrapes!"

"Worse than this?" Jimmy Joe couldn't believe that.

"I'm not saying that this isn't a bad one," Piper admitted. "But if I've learned anything, it's that you just got to keep moving forward and do what needs getting done. There isn't anyone who's going to do it for you."

"Piper, stop talking and save your strength." Conrad was supporting the other side of her. Jimmy Joe had watched him regularly check her vital signs as they traveled. Each time he did so, his face grew paler and his lips more tightly drawn.

"I'm fine," Piper insisted, only to have the red throbbing suddenly increase so that she bucked with the force of it and was pulled back into a fitful sleep.

Without the sun in the sky or anything else to mark the passing time, there was no way to know how long it was taking them. It felt like an eternity. Rory Ray had taken it upon himself to assume the lead position, and, marching in front of the group, he set the pace, reveling in the danger and dirt of it all.

"Halt!" he called, raising his arm in an L shape, his hand clenched into a fist.

"What's the problem?" Conrad called up.

"Come and see."

Conrad directed Jimmy Joe to a flat spot where Piper could safely rest. "You watch over her until I get back."

Next, he trotted up to the front of the group, where Rory Ray showed him how the cave had dead-ended.

"We've gone the wrong way. We've got to go back."

Conrad pulled at the collar around his neck. "No, no," he insisted. "This is the way out. I'm sure of it."

"You ain't thinking straight," Rory Ray said. "This can't be the way, because we can't walk through the mountain."

Conrad approached the cave and put his hands on it, allowing his fingers to feel the rocks. "This is the way. It has to be!" Conrad's brow twisted and furled in on itself. He angrily tugged at his thoughts. "I need a light!"

Rory Ray quickly pulled a small flashlight out of his pocket and flicked it on. Despite its small size, it was shockingly powerful. He directed the beam onto the cave wall in front, and instantly they could see the problem; they weren't being stopped by the side of the mountain—the wall in front of them had been built.

"Equilla finished her wall!" Conrad shook his head. "I should have known."

"You mean we're trapped in here?"

"Of course Equilla would seal us in," Kimber said angrily. "Like this is any surprise!"

Daisy lumbered up to the wall and, even though she still wore her collar, thrust several sturdy kicks at it that, under normal circumstances, would have easily sent the whole thing crashing down. But without her super strength, the stone didn't show a dent or mark.

"Stop, Daisy! You'll only hurt yourself." Conrad looked for other ways to take it down.

"Do we return to Mother Mountain?" Hanley asked with not a small amount of wishful hope in his voice.

"No, we find a way to break it down." Normally, Conrad would already have had a plan, but as he stood looking at the sheer rock in front of him, he didn't have a single thought.

"How?"

Uncomfortable silence followed. Looks were exchanged, shoulders shrugged, and foreheads furled up in contemplation.

"You know," Rory Ray said gruffly, "this one isn't that hard. Even I know what to do." He pulled a stick of dynamite out of the side pocket of his combat attire. "I'll take this baby down. There ain't a wall that dyna-mite can't take a bite out of."

Conrad reacted. "You were carrying dynamite? All this time?"

"Marines have to be prepared for anything." Rory Ray ran his hand over the wall, looking for the best place to lodge his arsenal, and pulled another stick out of his other shirt pocket.

Conrad held his hands in front of his chest like someone had a gun on him. "Well, I can't think of a better idea."

Rory Ray worked quickly to pick the best places to stage the explosives while the Chosen Ones watched in confusion.

"What is dine-might?" Kayla wondered aloud.

"Something we should get away from," Conrad said. "Everyone, move back!"

Conrad helped Jimmy Joe lift Piper. They carried her into the tunnels, moving past several turns and far away from the others. He wanted to take extra precautions with Piper because he couldn't anticipate how the explosion would affect her already unstable condition.

"Stay put until I come back." Conrad looked firmly into Jimmy Joe's eyes. "It's up to you to keep her safe."

"O-kay." There was a quaver in Jimmy Joe's voice.

As Conrad's footsteps receded, a quiet fell over Jimmy Joe, and he realized that his breath was coming out in frightened gasps.

"It's gonna be alright," Jimmy Joe said to himself. "It'll be just like Piper said—we'll find our way home."

The red light burned dangerously inside of Piper. What would he do if it got worse or she exploded?

As he sat in the dark, Jimmy Joe realized that this was

not at all what he thought it was going to be like when he imagined himself doing missions. More than that, he realized that he didn't want to be here: he wanted to go home. He liked the steady rhythm of farming and knowing what to expect, each day much like the one before. He liked the animals and the routine of it all and, truth be told, the quiet of the fields. If he ever got out of here, he was never going to leave Lowland County again.

It wasn't a sound that caught Jimmy Joe's notice but a movement of the dark. The dark itself shifted somehow and morphed, and then, in one heart-stopping moment, Elder Equilla stepped out of it, like a swimmer out of a pool, and was standing in front of him less than five horrifying feet away.

Jimmy Joe's throat closed tight, and his chest heaved.

Elder Equilla watched Jimmy Joe's distress with no discernable emotion on her face. Her hands were folded in front of her, her facial features arranged by serenity and a touch of mild curiosity. Jimmy Joe hadn't appreciated before how beautiful she was: her brow was regal; her eyes shone with wisdom and a hard elegance. Her body was sculpted in graceful lines and draped in the finest cloth.

"You are an Outsider," Elder Equilla stated, and instantly her gaze slid over him and down to Piper. "I have come to take Piper McCloud back to Mother Mountain. She is in need of our help: she's dying."

Jimmy Joe was not expecting this, and he forgot about himself enough to say, "She's dying?"

"It is certain. I can help her." Equilla took a step forward, but Jimmy Joe scrambled to his feet and opened his arms wide, shielding Piper. It was a feeble move in the face of someone so powerful, but it was all he could do.

"P-Piper wants to go home," he said, his voice faltering. "She wants to stop the bugs."

Equilla shrugged this off. "She is one of us. She must stay with her own kind."

"But . . . Piper was born and bred in Lowland County, so *we're* her kind."

Equilla dispatched Jimmy Joe's argument with a delicate flick of her fingers. "And did you treat her as one of your own?"

"She was tr-treated just fine," Jimmy Joe stammered, a guilty flush creeping up the side of his face. "Sure, some folks didn't approve of all her flying."

"Chosen Ones value what she is. You must understand that the wisdom of our people has shown that peace and happiness are only formed when like stays with like. It is the only way." Equilla's eyes softened suddenly. "I know what you want, Jimmy Joe." Equilla said his name carefully, dwelling on each syllable.

"H-how did you know my name?"

"I know many things. I know that deep inside you is the seed of a special ability." A shadow of a smile touched Equilla's lips. "Perhaps *you* should stay here too. There are those who could help you make that seed blossom, and then you, too, could be one of us."

"Me? I have a special ability?" A jolt burst across Jimmy Joe's skin, making the hairs on his arms and the back of his neck stand up straight. "Really?"

"It would need the encouragement of our most talented specialists to see it blossom. Only on Mother Mountain could that happen. There is nothing to fear when you live with us."

Jimmy Joe felt his chest rise as he breathed in Elder Equilla's dream for him. "But what about Piper . . ."

"If Piper returns to the Outside, she will fail. And after she fails, she will die." Equilla sighed sadly. "As her friend, you could be the one to save her. It is up to you, Jimmy Joe Miller. This is your moment to be a hero."

As Equilla said the word "hero," it traveled out of her lips and seemed to become a real, physical thing to Jimmy Joe. It sailed away from her like an arrow, and at the place it impacted his chest, it exploded into fiery energy that almost lifted him off his feet.

"Hero," Jimmy Joe breathed. Yes, he was a hero. He

felt his body lean toward Equilla like she was pulling him to her.

"You belong here, Jimmy Joe. This is your place. You are home."

Equilla reached out her hand, an invitation for Jimmy Joe to take it. Jimmy Joe's hand rose up. The way Equilla talked about Outsiders was so familiar. It reminded him of something . . .

Equilla's fingers fluttered in irritation. "Take my hand!"

As though drawn by an unseen force Jimmy Joe started to walk toward Equilla when a ruckus could be heard in the cave behind them. "Get down!" Rory Ray screamed. "Get down!"

"Outsiders are wicked and violent, and no good will ever come of them for you or Piper."

Jimmy Joe stopped dead. Equilla sounded just like his mother. He had heard his mother say just the same thing about Piper and her friends, and he had believed his mother, believed every word she had said.

"You need to listen to me, Jimmy Joe Miller. Come to me." Elder Equilla's voice was commanding. "Now!"

"No." Jimmy Joe's arms fell to his sides. "I think . . ." Jimmy Joe thought deeply and intently. "I think that if Piper wants to go home, then she should go home."

Equilla's eyes flashed; a red blush crept up into her

stoic face. "You are thoughtless and cruel—like all Outsiders. You could never have been one of us."

Suddenly, an explosion rocked the cave, dust billowing toward them like a wall of water. The rocks above Equilla tumbled and shattered. Rushing back to Piper, Jimmy Joe curled his body over her to protect her from the rocks. He covered his mouth to keep the dust out and waited like that until things got quiet again.

"Jimmy Joe!" Conrad, Rory Ray, and all the others came running to him.

"I blew that wall apart!" Rory Ray smirked. "You should see the hole I put in that sucker."

Conrad was right behind him, and even he had a smirk on his face. "It was quite the explosion."

Myrtle looked at the mounds of fallen rock that had miraculously not crushed the two of them, and she considered the boy in front of her with respect and appreciation. "You did good, Jimmy Joe Miller."

Jimmy Joe smiled.

Piper moaned loudly, the red light inside her all at once flaring up, angrily causing her body to buck.

"Let's get her home!" Jimmy Joe said, reaching to lift Piper. With Conrad's help, they gathered her up and ran.

CHAPTER

37

I$ T FELT TO PIPER LIKE THE REVERSE OF being born; instead of pushing her out into the world, the red light inside of her was sucking her into its core—an impossibly cramped space that was agonizingly tight. She fought and struggled against it, but it was relentless.

The sound was the first thing to change. The intense chirping that had been ringing in her ears started to morph, as though someone were carefully tuning a channel, dialing it to receive a station's coordinates. With a *pop*, the chirping became voices, thousands of voices crying out for help in a chorus.

Then silence.

Piper opened her eyes. She was hovering, suspended high above the earth. She could see oceans and continents and the clouds above them. It would have been incredibly peaceful, bobbing about, if her body hadn't been jammed into a space the size of a large beach ball. Even drawing air into her lungs was an effort, and her eyeballs were the only part of her body she could freely move.

Panic like hot lava was released into her veins. She struggled, pushing and pulling, on the brink of losing control.

"Ahhhhh."

"Stop that," said a voice. "Don't struggle."

The sound of the voice distracted Piper from her welling panic, and she moved her eyeballs, scanning the space around her. Her body was rotating slowly, and as she turned, she caught a quick glimpse of a bug flying near her. Then the moment she blinked, it was no longer a bug but instead a creature cramped up in its own enclosed small space just like hers. It was floating about thirty feet away, and then thirty feet on the other side of it was another creature, and so on and so on for as far as the eye could see.

"Did you say something to me?" Piper called out.

"If you fight against it, it'll only get tighter," the creature said. "You have to stay still."

"But I can't breathe," Piper panted. "It's so tight I can't even breathe."

"Take small sips of air. You must remain as small as you can."

Piper did as it instructed. With her rising sense of panic momentarily at bay, she was able to assess the creature in front of her. It was hard to actually describe it, since, like her, it was so scrunched up it wasn't possible to accurately identify what was what. It looked like it had a tail that was coiled around its body, and it was using two clawlike hands to pull the tail like a rope to hold itself in tightly. It had ears that were folded down and a long snout that was pushed onto its chest. Its eyes were twice as large as Piper's and had red pupils.

"What's your name?" Piper managed when she had collected up enough shallow breaths to form the words.

"Ninsa."

"Why can't I move?" Once again, Piper felt a rising panic inside her, the feeling that she might lose control entirely at any moment.

"I do not know. It has always been so."

"How do we get out of here?"

"Why would you want to get out?"

A cramp was budding in Piper's ankles and in her neck. She had rotated away, losing sight of Ninsa, and this filled her with fear.

"Ninsa? Ninsa? Can you hear me?"

"I can hear you."

The sound of his voice reassured Piper, and her breath came again. "How do we get out?"

"Remain still and be patient."

"For what?"

Ninsa didn't have an answer to this.

In the distance, a cry rang out, and Ninsa quickly closed his eyes. Piper looked past him to the source of the cry, where another scrunched-up creature like Ninsa suddenly exploded into red flames. Piper had to close her eyes to shield them from the power of the blast. When it was safe to open them again, nothing remained in the space that had once held the creature.

"Ninsa! Ninsa?"

"I am here."

"What just happened?"

"He grew. There was no more room for him. You must stay small."

Piper shivered. "But I'm growing. I can't help it. My body wants to grow."

Using her fingers, Piper rubbed against whatever it was that was holding her in. It was smooth and seamless and hard—an invisible prison. Next, she took her finger and poked it. Her fingernail created a hard tapping noise. She focused on that, using the nail like a small hammer. "There has to be something that will break this shell."

Ninsa could not think of anything and leaned into himself, squeezing tighter.

The force of another explosion that was felt but not seen caused them both to pause. "Ninsa," Piper said, "I live on a farm, and we have chickens, and when the chickens lay eggs, sometimes the baby chicks aren't able to peck their way out. How can I help you get out? How do you normally break out?"

"I do not know."

"Do you have claws? Or super strength? What exactly are you?"

Ninsa thought about it and said, "I am Ninsa. What are you?"

"I'm Piper McCloud."

"And what is Piper McCloud?"

Piper sighed. "I'm . . . well, I'm just a girl. Nothing special."

"I am the same."

"But no, you can't be. You were created with something special that you do so that you can break out of this shell."

Ninsa floated quietly, clutching himself. "Can you get out?"

The tapping of her fingernail had produced no results, and Piper was once again fighting an upswelling wave of claustrophobia. "I used to be able to fly," Piper panted. "That was my special thing. But I got bitten, and now I can't remember."

"All I remember is this." Coiling his tail even tighter, Ninsa felt the strain of staying small.

A wave of pain overtook Piper, and she could contain her panic no longer. "We must remember. We must fight!" With all her might she pushed against the shell, screaming as she did so.

"AHHHHHHH!"

CHAPTER

38

"SHE'S COMING BACK TO US."

Piper's eyes snapped opened to find Jasper leaning over her, his hands still glowing. She could feel herself panting and flailing about. Daisy rushed forward and held her down.

"Conrad," someone called.

Piper's panic was still cresting when Conrad came into view, looking down at her with concern.

"Con, Con." Piper's voice wasn't more than a rasp. "I saw them. I saw what they looked like, and it was just like you said: they are communicating with me."

"What are you talking about, Piper?"

"The bugs. I was with them. Somehow. I mean, I wasn't there physically, but it felt like I was there. And I was talking to one of them." Piper struggled to sit up.

Conrad nodded to Daisy, who released her hold and then leaned down to help Piper sit.

Now that she was partially upright, Piper could see that she had been carried back to Lowland County, and they were all in the old barn. It was dark but for the blue lights over the workstations and the glow from screens. All the workstations were buzzing, and the kids were working hard, rushing from station to station. Jimmy Joe and Rory Ray were in the mix with the Chosen Ones, and Piper could see a cluster of kids huddled around the team-meeting table scrutinizing a turning 3-D globe.

"We were afraid you weren't going to regain consciousness," Conrad said, leaning over the table where Piper was lying down so that he could check her pupils and her vital signs.

"It's like they're stuck inside shells, and they can't get out. And they aren't even trying, because they don't think it's possible." Piper felt like she must do something urgently. "We have to help them get out!"

"That's what we're trying to do, Piper." Conrad helped her down off the table. "We've made progress. C'mon—now that you're awake, we can have a team meeting."

As soon as Piper sat down in her chair, Lily was at her side and quickly filled her in on what had happened while she had been unconscious. They had rushed back to Lowland County, and as soon as they got there, they'd figured out a way to release their collars. Getting her powers back was the happiest moment of Lily's life.

"I can imagine." Piper wished it might have been so easy for her to get her flying back.

"We've been hard at work since we got back, and no one got any sleep last night," Lily yawned. "Bugs are going nuclear all around the planet, and when they go off in clusters, they take down the power grids in whole cities. Conrad says that we're at the tipping point."

By now everyone was gathered around the table, chairs pulled up and wedged into any available space to accommodate them all. Conrad took his place at the head of the table and was on his feet.

"We've been working with the Chosen Ones to trace the virus that Max used on the bugs," Conrad began. "Using the samples that we collected from the bugs, we were able to use our technology along with the Chosen Ones' knowledge of the past to piece together what happened. Irma?"

Conrad turned to Irma, and she got to her feet. She was a quiet girl but not meek. She took a handful of dirt out of a pouch she had hung around her neck, then spit into it and used her hands to shape it. When it was ready, she placed it on the table and blew on it. The mound of dirt looked like a lopsided spider, and as

Irma's breath came into it, the legs began to move, and it came to life.

"On Mother Mountain we do not have the name 'virus,'" she explained, guiding her dirt spider so that it didn't crawl away. "When there is a sickness, we create cures, tiny cures from the things that make up this earth. Generations ago many creatures in Xanthia were sick, and so a cure was created to help them. It looked like this." She held up the wiggling dirt spider. "But it was very tiny. Tiny enough that it could crawl into the smallest parts of a living thing."

"That's what I have inside of me?" Piper was horrified at the thought.

"No," Conrad said. "This virus helps your immune system. Someone took this virus and altered it. As you know, Max is wily, but he's not *that* smart. Certainly not smart enough to engineer a virus like this one or know how to alter it."

"This boy, Max," Irma agreed, "tricked us into making the virus different."

"Then Max took the altered virus and infected one of the bugs with it," Conrad continued. "The bugs were the perfect target; they have a hive mentality and work as a collective, constantly communicating with each other, giving information, and telling each other what to do. All Max needed to do was infect one of the bugs for all of them to be affected. This virus is very sophisticated. Think of it like a thought. The thought of this virus is 'don't.'"

"Don't?" Piper repeated.

"That's right. Don't. As in 'don't molt.' Or 'don't fly.' Or 'don't do whatever it is that you most need to do.'" Conrad reached out, activating the computer over the table. Instantly a strand of DNA spun in front of them. A little purple wiggly creature that was spiderlike in appearance materialized next to it. "That is the virus." Conrad pointed to the purple spider. "Now watch what it does."

The spider crawled over to the DNA, settling itself on a strand and wrapping its legs around it.

"Every strand of DNA is a piece of information. The virus targeted this piece and strangled it. You no longer have that information."

"So that's why I can't fly?"

"Yes," Conrad said. "Exactly. But the truth is you can fly; it's still there, but you just can't access it, because it's covered up. The same is true for the bugs."

"Ohhh." The strand of DNA twirled in front of Piper, casting brightly colored lights over her face. "So how are you going to save the bugs?"

"I can't," Conrad said flatly. "The only person who can save them is you."

"Me?" Piper looked around the table, all eyes on her.

"Because the bugs work as a hive, they communicate with each other, and now, because you were bitten, they are communicating with you, too. That is why you began to glow red when you were close to the bugs; they were sending you information. This communication is a two-way street, though, and if you were to tell them how to break free, they would."

"But . . ." Piper had barely followed Conrad's complex explanation. "How exactly would I do that?"

"By showing them how to defeat the virus."

"How would I defeat the virus?"

"Fly."

"Fly?"

"Yes, fly." Conrad sat down and folded his hands together in front of him. "By accessing the chromosome affected by the virus and turning the 'don't' into a 'do,' you will effectively kill it. As soon as you do that, you can transmit that information to the bugs, and they'll be able to do the same. They will learn from you. If they molt their shell, they won't blast, and the planet will be saved."

"But . . ." Piper's hands went to her head, and she held it for a moment. "But I'm normal now. You said so."

"That's not entirely accurate," Conrad said. "My initial information led me to believe that the superhero chromosome had been killed, but in actuality it's just dormant, or sleeping. All we have to do is wake it up. I have created a special serum that will temporarily shake the virus off, but it will be up to you to activate it once it's been released. If you can fly again, the bugs will be saved too."

While Conrad's explanation sounded simple, the practical application of it seemed impossible to Piper. "But what does that mean? How do I activate a dormant chromosome?"

"You turn the 'don't' into a 'do.'" Conrad came round the table to Piper. "A normal person wouldn't find a way to save her friends and unite two peoples. That is not normal. You are extraordinary, and your flying is a sign of that. You are the same person you always were. Just let yourself be the flier you are."

Piper thought back to all the things they had tried to make her fly. "I don't know . . ."

"You can. And as soon as you fly, you will save the world." Conrad looked down at the watch on his wrist. "You've got less than an hour."

CHAPTER

39

THE GRASS BEHIND THE BARN WAS coated in cold dew that reflected the beams of the rising sun, making it appear like sparkling diamonds had been tossed over the field. A group of more than twenty kids stood off to the side, their eyes fixed on Piper as she walked a distance away from them and into the center of the field. It was quiet. No one spoke. Piper could hear the rooster waking and crowing, the sounds of the cows lowing and the sheep bleating.

Her upper right arm stung from the injection that Conrad had just administered to her. He told her it would work quickly to cast off the virus that had attached itself to her cells, but it would be temporary, and it was up to her to get up in the sky fast. The act of flying itself would permanently kill the virus. She knew the bugs were above her in the sky where she could not see them, perilously close to exploding at any moment. The longer she waited, the more of them would die.

I can fly. I can fly.

Where was her flying inside her? Where had she put it?

Stark Raven had said, "Flying is something you do, not what you are." What did she mean by that? When Piper had been talking to Ninsa, he'd said that he couldn't remember what he was. What was she? Why did she fly?

Up. Up. Go up.

Nothing.

The eyes of the kids watching her from the edge of the field, their expectations and worry, burned into her. She could feel Conrad silently urging her on.

Fly. I can fly!

The soil on her shoes held her down.

The wind picked at her hair, blowing it in her face, and as she reached up to brush it away, her hand caught on the gold lily pin. She plucked it free, pulled it down, and turned it over in her hand so that the rays of the rising sun glinted off the gold. It was beautiful and shiny, but as she looked at it and felt the weight of it in her hand, Piper realized she actually didn't like it. She also didn't like the way it felt on her head: hard and heavy.

Dropping it on the ground, she pulled her hair back and twisted it into a rough braid, using one of the elastics around her wrist to tie it at the end.

Maybe she wasn't going to look the way she thought grown-ups ought to look. Things were not going to be so defined and clean for her. As much as she didn't like the messiness of her appearance and life, she was going to have to accept it and create her own version of what that looked and felt like.

With those thoughts sorted out inside her head, Piper closed her eyes one more time. She took a deep breath, filling herself with it, and slowly the glimmerings of a tingle ignited in her belly. It felt wild and free and uncontained. She leaned in and stoked it with breath after breath until the tingling became a forest fire of electricity and she was thrumming with it.

Yes, this is it. I remember now. This is how it felt. Like a release. Like the most natural thing in the world.

Piper didn't so much reach for the sky as embrace it, and instantly she rose up.

She ascended slowly.

At the side of the field, Conrad's hand became a fist, and he silently pumped it into the air. Jimmy Joe watched Piper fly with gladness and gratitude in his heart; he would never look at her flying again as anything less than the miracle that it was. The "oorah" that came out of Rory Ray's lips was more a prayer than a call to battle.

Twenty feet up, Piper's journey slowed and then stopped as her stomach began to burn hotly with the most piercing red light. Bursting out of her, it ignited like a star turning into a supernova. BOOM! She rocketed up, like lightning striking upward.

NINSA WAS HOLDING TIGHT, MAKING HIM-self as small as he possibly could, and the effort of that had become so tiring that he felt weak from it. His strength was failing him. Each moment felt like his last. He wouldn't be able to hold himself in for much longer.

BOOM!

He looked up as Piper's explosive red wave washed over him, passing through his every cell. As it did so, his mind began to feel a poke, and then suddenly there was a *pop* inside of it, and all at once he knew what he was.

He remembered that he was meant to hatch, not remain coiled up in a tiny ball. He was not a small thing: he was destined to be a big thing. And he wanted to be what he was.

Releasing himself, he felt the terrible pressure of the small space he was cramped inside, and he let out a cry, but it turned into fire. His fire hit the egg and easily broke through it, shattering it apart.

Ninsa uncoiled his scaly body, released his tail, and flung apart his wings. Opening his mouth, he roared!

Across the sky in every direction, Ninsa's transformation and release was felt inside every egg. Like firecrackers, they began to burst.

———— ·◆· ————

MAX HAD CHOSEN A FRONT-ROW SEAT TO view the end of the world. It was a show he had no intention of missing. At the top of the Empire State Building, he had positioned his chair at just the right angle, his chilled soda in its cupholder. It was the perfect place to watch the impending explosions in the sky above and then the resulting effects on the city below.

"It's a good day for it."

Max couldn't agree with himself more. "We're in for quite a show."

"This'll be one for the history books!" Max indulged in a long suck on his soda and then smacked his lips together. "This is the one they'll remember you for, Max."

"You got that right."

When the electricity went out, when the cell phones went down and the computers failed, people would be shocked, disoriented, maybe even a little bit angry. But that would soon pass, and it would turn to panic and then fighting and looting. Without power and working equipment, the hospitals would shut down. Without cars, people would be stranded. Without technology, the police would be helpless.

Ahhh, yes. Things would be just the way Max liked them: completely out of control.

Above him, Max watched the first bug explode, a flash of white light in the sky. If you hadn't been looking for it and didn't know what it meant, it would have been easy to miss. Seconds later, there was a domino effect, a cascading burst of popping white lights, spreading like a wave outward.

"This is it." Max rubbed his hands together gleefully, giggling. "Here it comes!"

He waited.

And waited.

And waited some more.

To Max's astonishment, the horns of the taxis on the New York streets did not grow silent; the lights in the buildings did not dim; there was neither silence nor pandemonium. In fact, nothing at all changed.

Slowly getting to his feet, his face a mask of confused disbelief, he leaned against the railing, pressing himself as close as he could get, as though the extra inches would suddenly show him the world picture he expected and needed to see.

Absolutely nothing had changed.

"But this can't be!" Max looked up and down. "They exploded. I saw them explode." Max threw up his hands. "This isn't fair!"

A couple with a small child who also happened to be on the Empire State Building's observation deck moved away to what they hoped was a safe distance from the strange boy who was talking to himself.

"This was supposed to be the end of the world," Max wailed.

More people moved away. Security began to gather.

Max grabbed his hair, pulling on it. "I want destruction. It was the perfect plan. I did everything right. I WANT CHAOS!" Max lashed his fists against the metal bars petulantly.

"Young man, I'm going to have to ask you to stop doing that," a beefy security guard said with a practiced calm and careful voice.

"Get away from me. You have no idea who you are dealing with. It was those kids—Piper and Conrad." Max pointed to the security guard as though it were his fault, as though he were in league with Piper and Conrad and had aided and abetted them. "They've ruined my perfect plan."

"It's okay, kid. Plans change." The security guard didn't make any sudden moves but edged closer. "When you get to be my age, you'll understand that things turn out the way they do for a reason. No point getting upset about it."

As the security guard's words hit Max, his eyes snapped into focus. He regarded the man, seeing him. "Plans change?"

"Sure they do. I tell my son that all the time. If it doesn't work out, you just got to keep trying. And maybe if you don't get what you want the first time around, it's because there's something better waiting for you."

"Something better?"

The security guard could see that Max was calming down, and he relaxed his shoulders. "Sure. You're young. You can do anything you want. You got a bright future ahead of you. Just keep trying."

"Yes." Max nodded, his chin getting firm. "That's just what I'll do. I underestimated them—that was my problem. But that's okay, because challenges are fun, and I like fun."

The security guard chuckled. "Heck, everyone likes fun."

Max chuckled too, but his laugh was menacing and dangerous. "Want to see something fun?"

"Sure, kid."

Spinning around, Max threw himself at the metal fence and, with two movements, reached the top.

"Hey! Hey!" The security guard was right behind him, but Max was out of reach.

"I already know what I'll do next!" Max gave the security guard a Cheshire cat grin.

"Get down from there! You got the whole rest of your life in front of you."

"Don't I know it! And I'm going to enjoy every second of it too." Max ripped open his jacket, revealing a harness around his waist. With a quick click, he snapped his carabiner onto a tether that had been sneakily hidden out of view.

"Stop! You're gonna get yourself in trouble doing that. There are rules." Now the security guard was reaching for his radio.

That was the thing about living forever: you never had to worry about consequences or rules. "The only rules I'm gonna follow"—Max grinned—"are the rules of having fun. I intend to have *a lot* of fun! And nobody, not you or Piper or Conrad, is going to stop me."

Pushing off, Max rappelled down the Empire State Building. It wasn't as good as watching the end of the world, but it was still pretty darn good.

IN XANTHIA, AT THE TOP OF MOTHER Mountain, Elder Equilla looked up, feeling the emergence of the bugs from their shells.

Pursing her lips, she clasped her hands and looked out over the valley. Just like the Fortune Flier had said, this was the harbinger of great change. A new day was dawning.

Elder Equilla did not like it.

But she was ready to fight it. Placing her hand over her heart, she silently vowed to build another wall. This time, it would be stronger and safer; this time, no one would break through it. She would prepare her people for what was to come using all measures at her disposal to keep them away from the Outsiders. This she would do with every breath in her body.

Asanti.

EVEN FROM THE GROUND, IT WAS POSSIBLE to see a burst of light each time an egg cracked open. Conrad craned his neck and squinted his eyes, but he couldn't see what had emerged.

"Smitty? Smitty, are you seeing this?"

Smitty was shaking his head. "You know I am. You

aren't going to believe this! You know what's coming out of those eggs?"

Conrad waited for Smitty to tell him.

"They look like dragons. Baby dragons. But dragons all the same." Smitty could barely trust his own eyes. "Does that make any sense?"

Conrad smiled. "It makes sense to me."

<hr>

IN THE END, SAVING THE WORLD AS WE know it was a quiet task accomplished on a normal day in a meadow, where one girl, not particularly beautiful or smart, but like most other girls in every way, managed to do something extraordinary.

Standing alone, but watched on all sides by kids from different places who had learned to work together, she threw up her arms and believed that she could fly—despite all evidence to the contrary and in spite of a voice inside her that said strongly and firmly "don't." She did it anyway.

CHAPTER

40

*T*HINGS GOT CROWDED BACK IN LOWLAND County; instead of eleven extraordinary kids at the McCloud farm, there were now almost twenty. Not only that, but the Miller kids started spending a lot of time there too. Word spreads fast in a place like Lowland County, and once Rory Ray and Jimmy Joe got to talking to other kids and telling them that there was nothing wrong with Piper McCloud's head, they came to see for themselves. Their parents wouldn't believe a word of the rumors that were being spread around, but the kids were willing to take a look, and soon enough they started to stop by the McCloud farm and play for a while.

The Chosen Ones decided not to go back to Xanthia right away and instead stayed in Lowland County to learn more about the Outsiders. The Outsiders were nothing like what they had been told, and the more they learned, the more questions they had. No sooner were they good and settled at the farm than Joe McCloud's old pickup truck rolled into the yard. The sight of her parents sent Piper into a fever of excitement.

"Ma! Pa!" Piper flung herself at the truck door, pulling it open and hugging her mother. "Are you okay, Ma?"

"Well, I'm not the first person on this planet to have a baby, and I won't be the last." Betty patted Piper's back as she hugged and hugged her. "I think maybe I won't go and have another baby after this one, though. There's a time for everything, and my baby time is up."

Baby Jane was sleeping in her car seat. Piper cooed and whispered over her and gently touched the top of her head. "She's the most beautiful thing I've ever seen. Can I hold her, Ma? Can I bring her inside?"

"Don't see why not."

Joe came around and helped his wife out of the truck, and Piper took the car seat with baby Jane sleeping inside. Gathered on the porch were all the kids, half of whom Betty had never seen before.

"Well, it looks like we've got visitors," Betty sighed.

Being on a farm with these kids meant there was never a dull moment. "Let me get settled and put the kettle on, and then I'd better hear all about what's been going on around here."

For the rest of the day Piper gazed upon, cuddled, fed, and sang to her sister, Jane. Jane was a good baby. She didn't scream or cry but instead looked around at the world with thoughtful and serious eyes. She liked looking at Piper, probably because Piper lit up like a lightbulb anytime she was close to her.

"I think she's the best baby in the world," Piper said that night as she watched Jane sleeping in her crib. "I don't think there's a better baby anywhere."

"She looks pretty much like every other baby," Betty mused, cocking her head to see her. "But, come to think of it, she looks just like you did at that age. The spitting image."

Both Betty and Piper had the same thought at the same time, but neither of them dared give voice to it.

What would happen if Jane turned out to be a flier too? Piper thought about going through all the things she had been through to learn how to fly and find her place in the world as a flier. Flying was a lot of fun, but it was also a big responsibility; after all, from those to whom much is given, much is expected. Did she want that for her little sister? She was definitely going to be keeping a close eye on Jane from now on.

"Well," Betty sighed, "Jane's a good name. Sensible and plain."

"Yes," Piper agreed. "Jane's a good name."

CHAPTER

41

$\mathcal{J}$T WAS A CLEAR, COOL NIGHT THAT DIS-played the stars to their best advantage on the evening of the Lowland County Spring Dance. The Lindviks' barn was decked out with paper lanterns and garlands of wildflowers wrapped around the posts, as well as a large candelabra with beeswax candles that cast a flickering glow over the rafters. A long table with a red-checkered tablecloth groaned with punch and dainty tarts and other goodies, while the Straitharn brothers, who had wrestled themselves into shirts and ties, were fiddling up a storm. Dottie Dutton had been coaxed into sitting at the piano, for she had a reputation for tickling the ivories, and she proudly wore her prom dress, which still fit her but stank of moth balls.

In the end, Betty had relented, since the dress Lily had made for Piper was ruined at Stonehenge, and took Piper down to Jameson's store. The dress they found and that Piper loved wasn't as fashionable as the one Lily had designed, but somehow it was just the perfect one for her. It was robin's-egg blue with sparkly stones randomly encrusted about the full skirt and at the top of the neckline so that when the light hit them, they glowed. Lily had begged Piper to allow her to do her hair, but Piper declined the help—she wanted to look like herself, not like a fashion plate. She washed her hair with special lavender shampoo and brushed it until it shone. Gathering up the pieces at both sides, she fixed them on top of her head and tied them with a simple bow. The rest she let hang loose down her back, and it was so springy and clean that it flowed with each step she took.

When she came down the stairs and Joe caught sight of her, he got tears in his eyes.

"You look beautiful," Joe said.

Piper twirled for him and then hugged him tight.

Betty, who was holding baby Jane, sniffed loudly at such a display. "I don't approve of all these goings-on," she said. "Youngens going off to dances at night, it's not right."

Moments later, when Piper hugged her and baby Jane, Betty got misty eyed and quickly excused herself to change the baby's diaper, fearing that calamity would surely strike if she didn't.

Conrad had asked Piper to the dance.

Piper had said yes.

She hadn't been expecting him to ask. She was so happy to be flying again and spending time with Jane that there was little room in her mind to think about such things. In fact, she'd forgotten all about the dance. She had been sitting on the porch swing, holding Jane in her arms and singing to her when Conrad had fumbled up, leaning against a post, then decided not to lean, then shifted back and forth, not sure what to do with his hands.

"I've been looking for you," he said.

"Jane just smiled at me," Piper said, not bothering to look up. "And Ma says I can't fly with her, which makes absolutely no sense if you ask me."

"Jimmy Joe asked AnnA to the dance," Conrad interjected.

"I wasn't going to fly high or fast, just a little ways off the ground. I don't think it's too dangerous," Piper continued. "I think Jane would like it, don't you?"

Conrad thought that flying with a newborn was problematic but didn't think it wise to point that out. Instead he said, "The dance is this weekend. That's three days away, or seventy-four hours and thirty-three minutes."

Jane let out a gurgle, and, delighted by it, Piper started to sing to her again.

"Piper?"

"Um-hmmm."

"I would be honored—" Conrad cleared his throat. "What I mean to say is, will you accompany me to the dance?"

The song died in Piper's mouth, and she looked up at Conrad. He was flushed, and now that she was paying attention, she saw that he had carefully combed his hair and put on a crisp shirt that made his eyes look bluer then normal and his mouth more earnest.

"I know you said you wouldn't go with me," Conrad continued. "But I thought perhaps you might change your mind. I would like to take you to the dance, if you'd like to come with me." The flush on his face deepened as he waited on Piper's response. "Will you?"

Piper sat very still and thought about how she felt about going to the dance with Conrad. She was surprised to discover that she felt not jittery or uncomfortable but happy. To spend an evening with her best friend at a party seemed like the most natural thing in the world. She did not know how she felt about Conrad beyond that, other than that they were best friends, and that was okay too. She didn't need to know that now; it wasn't important. There would be time to figure that out later.

"I will go to the dance with you," she said. "I'd like that." And then she started to float.

⸺ ◆ ⸺

ON THE NIGHT OF THE DANCE, CONRAD WORE a perfectly tailored blue suit with a dapper bow tie. He'd allotted many hours of the remaining seventy-four before the dance to practicing steps so that when they were on the dance floor, he twirled and whirled Piper until her skirts ballooned out like the petals of a flower in full bloom.

Piper also danced with Jimmy Joe when he wasn't dancing with AnnA, and with Rory Ray, who didn't ask anyone to the dance because he said he was too busy getting ready to go off to basic training.

It was agreed by everyone that Lily Yakimoto was the most elegant of all in an ivory silk gown of her own design, beaded liberally with pearls. Millie Mae Miller took one look at Lily and sniffed loudly, commenting to those close by that it was shocking the way a child her age was rigged up in such a fashion. Millie Mae went on to say that she would not put anything past those youngens at the McCloud farm, and then made ominous predictions about how they were up to no good.

It was surprising to Millie Mae that the matrons closest to her were not particularly interested in what she had to say and made excuses to move away from her after that. They had been hearing different stories from their children lately about what was going on at the McCloud farm, and while they weren't exactly sure what to believe, they were no longer blindly taking Millie Mae's word for it.

During a refreshment break, Hanley, Mayla, Kayla, and Asher cornered Conrad and peppered him with endless questions about everything from Outsider clothing to Outsider food to the way the dance steps worked. Taking the opportunity to get some fresh air, Piper drifted outside to enjoy the stars. It was such a night, and the stars called to her. After the dance was over and she'd changed out of her dress, she would slip out and fly under those stars.

"The birds have been telling me that you're flying again," said a voice.

Piper turned at the sound to see Stark Raven emerge out of the trees at the side of the barn. She was wearing a party dress, of sorts. It was bright orange, and she'd complemented it with a purple hat, upon which perched a chipmunk. She was wearing long gloves and sparkling silver shoes. In her hand was a crystal glass containing a green liquid that bubbled and smoked. Toasting Piper with the glass, she took a long draw from it and then smacked her lips.

"It's good to see you back up in the sky," Stark Raven said. "It's where you belong."

Piper raised her glass of punch to Stark Raven and toasted her back. "Thanks for all you did."

"I was just one piece of the puzzle." Stark Raven shrugged. "We all got a piece. It was you that put the pieces together."

"I had a lot of help," Piper admitted.

"That's not a bad thing. Some puzzles are more difficult than others. I wouldn't be nothing without my friends."

The chipmunk on Stark Raven's head began to flick his tail and chuckle.

"Keep your fur on," Stark Raven said, looking up toward him. "We're going, we're going. Well, I'd best be on my way. There's a party, and we're late."

Piper moved aside so that Stark Raven could go into the barn. "I didn't know you came to dances."

"Ha! Wouldn't be caught dead at that thing. No, there's a real humdinger by the stream. Those badgers know how to throw shakers. Don't think you'd like it, though."

Stark Raven melted back into the forest without so much as a good-bye. Piper could only imagine what sort of forest party Stark Raven was going to. No doubt it involved worms, rocks, groundhogs, and birds.

In the barn behind her, the fiddles started up a waltz, and Conrad poked his head out. "May I have this dance, Miss McCloud?"

Piper glowed. "You may."

Taking Conrad's hand, she let him lead her onto the dance floor, and she made her absolute best attempts to keep her feet from floating off the ground as they danced the night away. She was only partly successful.

ACKNOWLEDGMENTS

WRITING THIS BOOK TAUGHT ME THREE THINGS . . .

Without my sister Kim I'd be lost.

Jodi Reamer is not only a fighter, she is also steadfast and loyal. Also, she deserves a medal for putting up with me.

Liz Szabla is quite possibly the most patient person in the world. Ditto the need for a medal.

Piper McCloud has lived in my head and my heart for a considerable amount of time. I am so happy that she finally got the ending she deserved.